Banjo and Swift

By Iacovos Le Du

This Book © Iacovos Le Du, 2021
Illustrations © Yoan Vezenkov

All rights reserved

Independently published via Kindle Direct Publishing

Disclaimer: the graphic art of the author's silhouette herein belongs to the author. All other illustrations are by Yoan Vezenkov, produced for the purposes of this publication.

I would like to thank James McPhee and Joschua Knüppe for their invaluable contributions towards enhancing the scientific sections of this book. I also want to thank Maria Christou and Spiros Derveniotis for their constructive help and feedback throughout the process of developing this story, and Ronan Le Dû for key help in the legal completion of this book.

Effort has been taken to make this book as scientifically accurate as possible, and over 25 scientific publications relevant to this story were consulted (most of which are listed at the end of this book). However, there are two reasons for which long-lasting scientific accuracy cannot be guaranteed for any aspect of this story.

Firstly, there are major gaps in our current understanding of prehistoric life in general, and of the animals and environments displayed in this book. To be able to tell this story, speculation and creative choices have been made to fill in these gaps – where possible, these will be noted later in the book.

Secondly, science is an ever-changing field of study, and palaeontology is one area in which this is most true. The information contained here may very well be outdated within months or even days of this book's publication. But that is the beautiful nature of science, and this book should be treated as nothing more than a window into the research conducted at the time of the book's publication.

Contents

The Animals 3
The Plants 11
Part One 17
    Chapter 1 19
    Chapter 2 22
    Chapter 3 25
    Chapter 4 30
    Chapter 5 34
Part One: The Science 47
Part Two 55
    Chapter 1 57
    Chapter 2 63
    Chapter 3 67
    Chapter 4 71
    Chapter 5 77
Part Two: The Science 87
Part Three 95
    Chapter 1 97
    Chapter 2 104
    Chapter 3 108
    Chapter 4 113
    Chapter 5 118
    Epilogue 131
Bibliography 137

The Animals

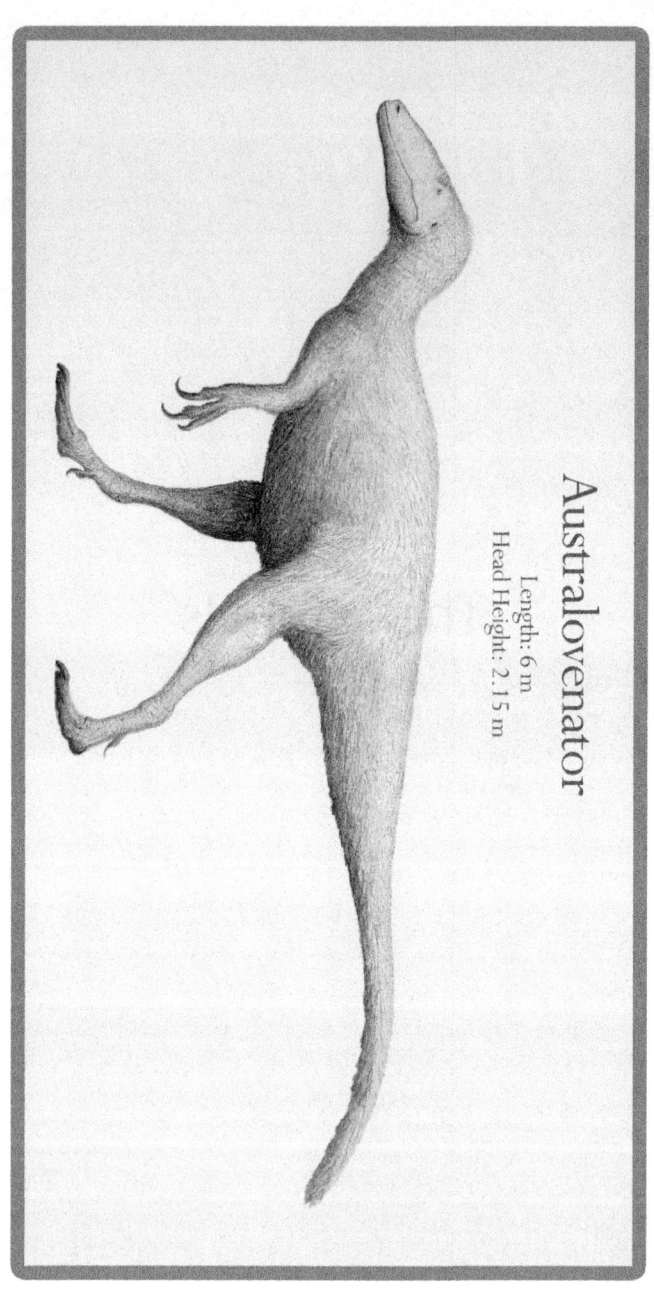

Australovenator
Length: 6 m
Head Height: 2.15 m

Ornithopod
Length: 1.5 m
Head Height: 60 cm

Savannasaurus
Length: 15 m
Head Height: 6.3 m

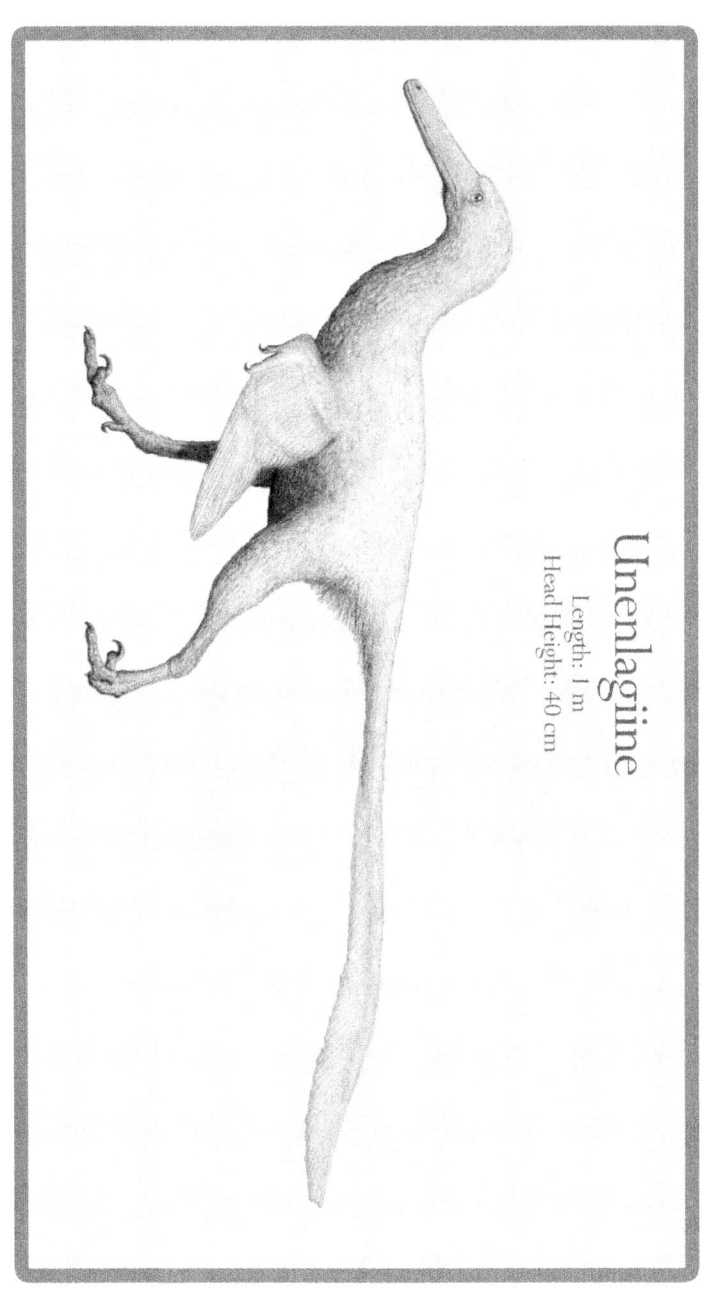

Unenlagiine
Length: 1 m
Head Height: 40 cm

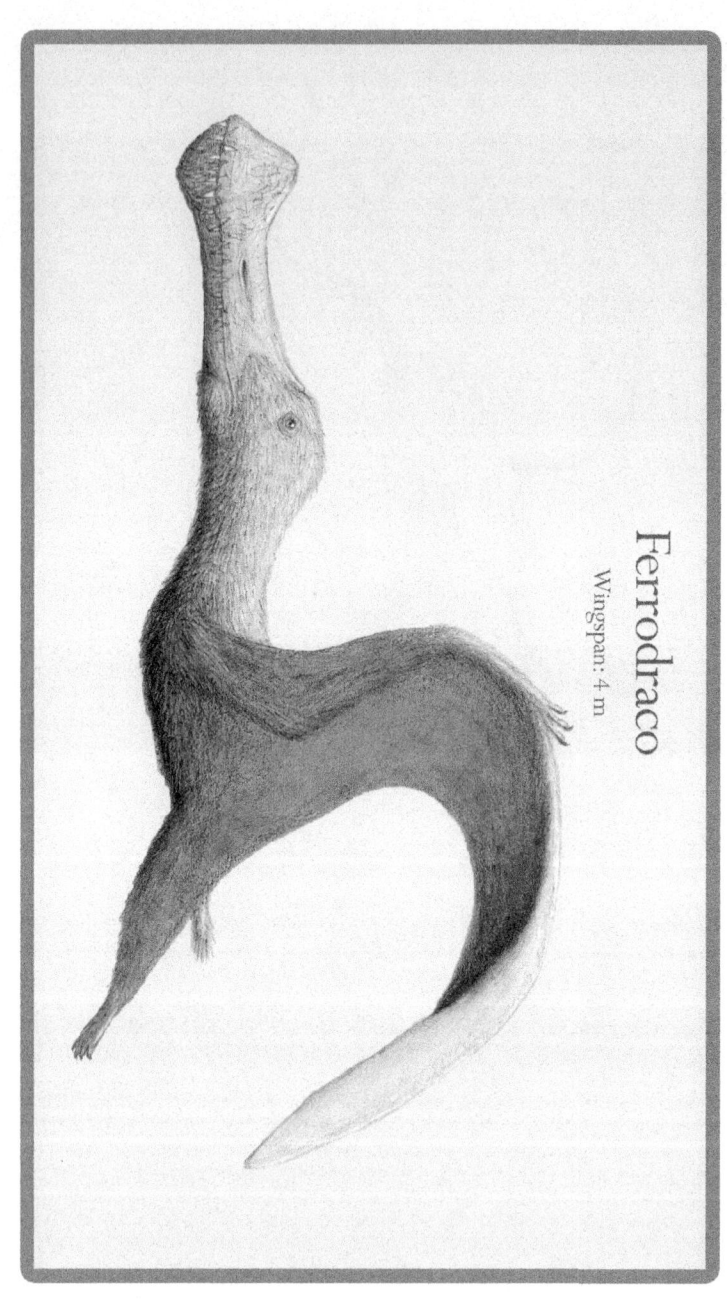

Ferrodraco
Wingspan: 4 m

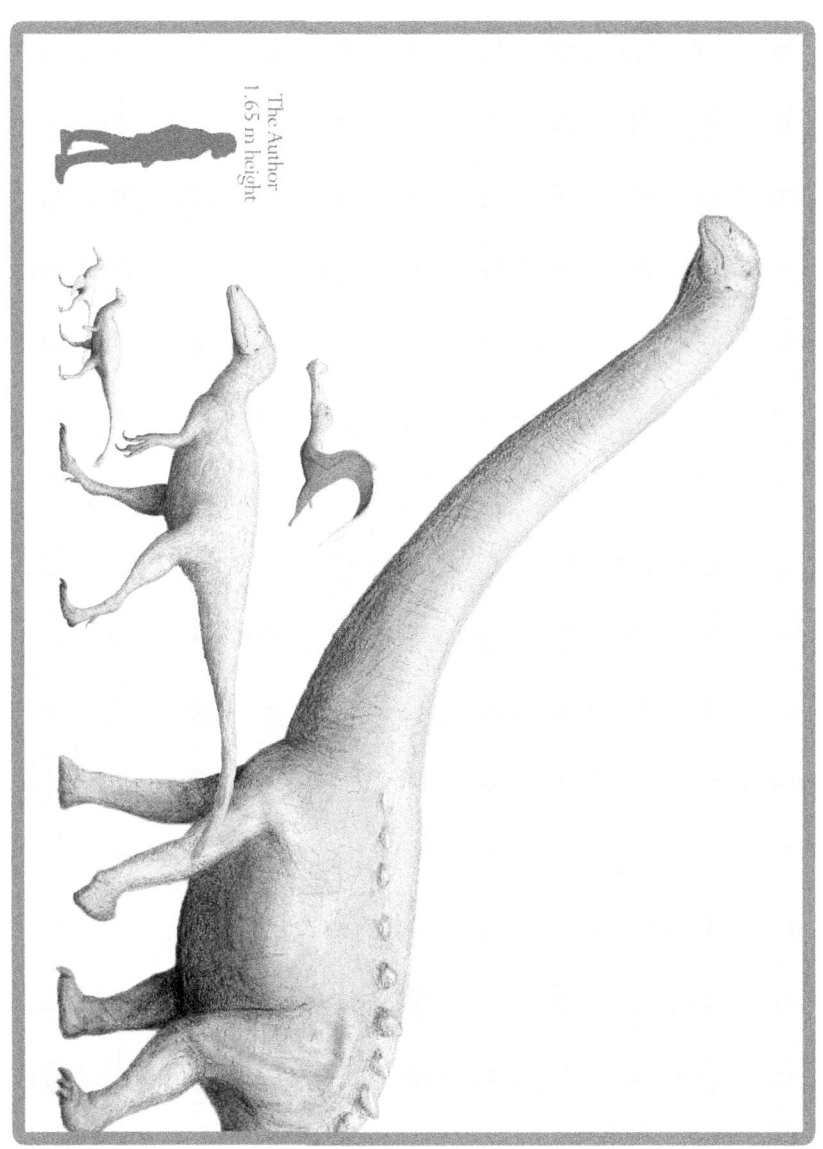

The Plants

Ginkgo
Height: Possibly up to 30 m

Conifer
Height: Possibly up to 40 m

Lovellea wintonensis (flowering plant)
Height: Possibly up to 30 m

Cycad

Height: Possibly up to 4 meters

Part One

Chapter 1

Midday. The sun rises in the sky. Temperatures soar, and the shadows of the tall, podocarp conifer trees shrink and fade, leaving little shade on the forest floor. A river, in full flow after yesterday's rains, cuts through the forest. Its waters are cool and tempting to the forest animals seeking some escape from the summer heat. Still, they know better than to venture into the rivers: small crocodiles, known as Isisfordia, lurk beneath the waters. Ordinarily, they hunt fish, but would not pass up the opportunity to get a quick meal, should an animal enter the river to cool down.

One Isisfordia lounges on the river bank, soaking up the sun's warmth. She has already eaten her fill today. The fish are plentiful and easy to catch. Her long, wide toothy jaw hangs open, as she pants heavily. She, too, is trying to cool down, and letting air flow through her mouth is a quick way to lower her body temperature.

She remains on constant alert. Despite her armored body that offers her some protection, she is only a meter long, and there are dangers in these forests. Large carnivores, meat-eaters, who would not pass up the opportunity to ambush an Isisfordia.

Suddenly, a twig snaps and leaves rustle, as something approaches the riverbank. She whips around, nervously, looking for the source of the noise.

Then, out of the forest and onto the riverbank, steps a dinosaur.

6 meters long, it stands 2 meters tall on two very strong, very long legs. Its body is low-slung and horizontal and covered in a light coat of reddish-brown feathers. Behind its legs is a long tail. Held out horizontally, it counterbalances the weight of its body, its long, powerful arms, and its head and neck.

The head and neck are both long, and the head sports a jaw lined with sharp teeth designed for cutting up meat. The first two of its three fingers are tipped with long, sharp claws, curved like hooks. From head to toe, this animal is designed to be the ultimate meat-eating dinosaur. A perfect predator. And its name is Australovenator.

The Australovenator marches towards the river. The Isisfordia decides to not take any chances and runs off. The Australovenator watches as she disappears into the water in a splash, sending out ripples.

The Australovenator is not in the mood to hunt; she has already done that. In her hands, she carries her next meal: a small Ornithopod dinosaur, which she has just killed. She drops it as she bends down to the river's surface, and, opening her mouth, takes several big gulps of the water.

Her thirst quenched, she reaches down, picks up the Ornithopod, and carries it off with her as she leaves the riverside. A few moments pass and the Isisfordia comes back out of the water and resumes basking in the sun.

The Australovenator continues marching through the forest, her kill in her hands. Hunger gnaws within her, but the kill is not for her. She has mouths to feed.

Eventually, she reaches her destination: a small clearing in the forest. In the shade of a tree, two small dinosaurs lie. Her children. Two brothers, Banjo and Swift.

Once they see her, they get up, excitedly, and rush towards her, letting out welcoming calls. They are both smaller than she is, only 4 meters in length, but they still have the features of a deadly predator. The massive claws, the long legs. The only thing they lack is experience.

Their mother drops the kill down in front of them. Excitedly, they begin feeding, tearing into the carcass. The mother sits down a few meters away and waits. She will eat when they have finished feeding. She yawns and lays her head down. She does not need to watch over them; there is nothing in these forests that could pose a threat to them. Content, she closes her eyes and lets herself sleep, as the sound of her children eating continues.

About an hour later, she wakes. Her children sleep, well-fed and tired in the stifling heat. Hunger is what has awoken the mother, and she goes to the carcass and begins feeding herself. Their appetites almost equalling hers, her children have not left her much meat. She devours what remains of the Ornithopod, but her hunger is not fully satiated. As Banjo and Swift approach adulthood, she will struggle more and more to provide food for all three of them. Soon, it will be time to start preparing her children to hunt for themselves, and, in time, to leave the nest and forge their own path.

She turns and casts them one last look before the summer laziness overcomes her too. Banjo's head rests on his younger brother's neck, as they lie blissfully. She closes her eyes and joins them in sleep.

Chapter 2

Late afternoon. The Isisfordia lies on the riverbank. She prefers to hunt in the early morning and evening hours and will wait for the sun to start setting before returning to the water. Other Isisfordia are also gathered on either side of the river. The social life of the Isisfordia is rough and inconsistent. Sometimes they will tolerate each other and form small groups as they bask; other times, they may be irritable and keep their distance.

The Isisfordia is particularly irritable today. There is no precise reason for it, she is just on edge today. She contemplates going back into the water, but she decides to wait a little longer, still feeling lazy from the warm day.

Suddenly, she hears something behind her, and bursts into life, spinning around and hissing angrily.

In the shade of the trees, Swift stands. Over a meter tall, he towers over the small crocodyliform. Swift looks at her, curious, as she stands in front of him, jaws open and letting out a long low hiss.

Swift decides to advance, and the Isisfordia backs away slightly, daunted by his size. Swift interprets this as him having the upper hand, and decides to move even closer. The Isisfordia snaps, lunging forward and clapping her jaws shut. Swift staggers back, caught off guard.

The Isisfordia runs towards him, hissing. Swift steps back, intimidated by this small yet very aggressive creature. He then remembers that he is quite a bit larger than her, and decides to retaliate, snapping at her with his jaws. The Isisfordia backs off, and a sort of dance then begins between the two of them, each pushing the other back a bit before the other retaliates.

Eventually, Swift uses his longer reach, thanks to his height, to lean over and bite the Isisfordia on her back. The Isisfordia is enraged, not with pain, but with frustration, and lunges, biting Swift on the leg. Swift yelps in pain and kicks her away. The Isisfordia falls on her back, and she quickly wriggles back onto her front. Slightly hurt, but only more angered, the Isisfordia continues the assault, lunging and biting at Swift. Swift hops back nimbly, narrowly avoiding the Isisfordia's attacks.

He lashes out with his hand, hitting the Isisfordia on the snout, but he doesn't even dent the armored keratin on her face. The Isisfordia darts forward with impressive speed and nips Swift on the shin. Swift pulls back and starts to think he may have taken on more than he can chew. If he had the experience, he would know how to kill an Isisfordia, but he is clueless as to what to do with this small biting thing that won't stop hissing.

The other Isisfordia become interested in the commotion and start hissing. They are practically looking for a fight at this point. Swift hisses loudly, but the Isisfordia nipping at his feet doesn't care. His back to the river, and with the other Isisfordia getting to their feet, Swift is starting to get worried.

Suddenly, Banjo charges onto the riverbank. The other Isisfordia are taken aback, and lie back down. The Isisfordia tussling with Swift stops and turns towards Banjo, letting out an angry, throaty hiss.

Banjo rushes her, and she backs off, jaws still open. When he gets close, she lunges, but Banjo deftly avoids her strike. Swift hisses too, and the Isisfordia realizes it is greatly outmatched. Before either Australovenator can do anything, she turns and gallops back towards the river and into the water.

As the ripples fade, Swift turns to his brother. Moving towards him, they nuzzle affectionately. Swift has been saved. Granted, he was never in any real danger – the worst the Isifordias could have done would be to inflict minor injuries on his legs, but Swift is grateful nonetheless.

Together, they leave the riverbed and head back to the clearing they call home.

Chapter 3

Twigs snap underfoot as a dinosaur moves through the forest. It is small, only 1.5 meters long, and belongs to the Ornithopod group of dinosaurs. Like the Australovenators, it is bipedal. Its arms are short and five-fingered. Its snout is short too, and at the tip, it has a beak, used for nipping plants. This herbivore is covered in a thick coat of thin, primitive feathers, inherited from an ancestor which it shares with all other dinosaurs, including Australovenator.

The Ornithopod wanders through the forest, moving in and out of the shadows. A beetle crawls out in front of it. Small, but fat and juicy. The Ornithopod stops and watches it. Although it is primarily a plant-eater, like most plant-eaters it will not refuse a bit of protein in its diet. In one swift move, it reaches down and snaps up the beetle, crushing it in its beak.

The Ornithopod continues on its way. It is not searching for food, as there is plenty of that in the forest, in the form of the needle-like leaves of the conifer trees, or the thick green ferns that grow on the ground. This Ornithopod is looking for others of its kind. Ornithopods are a sociable species, and they enjoy each other's company, sometimes forming large flocks around watering holes and open areas.

From one such open area come noises of other Ornithopods, and this is what is luring the Ornithopod out of the relative safety of the forest. In a wide, grassless field, a large clearing in the woods, a flock of Ornithopods is gathered. In the midday heat, they loll about lazily. Young juveniles frolic and play with each other, under the watchful eyes of their kin.

A group stands alert, however, rearing back to raise their heads as high as possible and get as good a view of all that is around them. There can be no real peace for these herbivores. Due to their small size and relatively defenseless bodies, they are often viewed as an easy meal and must be wary.

Nevertheless, the field is calm and quiet, for now. The Ornithopod emerges from the forest, and a couple of others run up to greet it.

Suddenly, trees can be heard shaking. Leaves rustle, and branches creak and snap. The Ornithopods jump up, tense. Something is heading their way. Something big. The young Ornithopods stop playing and look around. For them, it is not a cause for fear, but a new phenomenon that fascinates them.

Indeed, none of the Ornithopods need to be worried. What approaches is not a threat – at least, not unless it steps on one of them. Into the field emerges a Diamantinasaurus. A type of dinosaur belonging to the group known as Titanosaurs, Diamantinasaurus is massive. 15 meters in length, and 15 tons in weight, it walks on four thick legs. Its tail is long and muscular; if swung, it could deliver an enormous blow to any dinosaur foolish enough to attack it. However, unless provoked, Diamantinasaurus is a peaceful herbivore. Its long neck allows it to reach leaves no matter how high or low they are, and it can swing its neck to browse from many different trees without even moving its body. Its head is small, and the needle-like teeth are only for stripping leaves from branches, not for chewing. All food goes straight to the massive gut, un-chewed and un-cut. Not needing to chew means it can spend all its time swallowing more and more food to fuel its massive body.

Realizing the Diamantinasaurus will most likely not pose a threat, the Ornithopods calm down, and return to their frolicking and resting. They are unaware that, this whole time, they are being watched.

Hidden in the trees' shadows, the mother Australovenator watches. The Ornithopods are her kind's favorite prey. It is no coincidence that both Australovenators and Ornithopods are perfectly built for speed and agility. An evolutionary arms race, with these two types of dinosaurs pushing each other to become faster and more agile. The Ornithopods still have the upper hand when it comes to agility, thanks to their small size and lower center of gravity. The Australovenator's stride length, however, gives it the upper hand in a straight chase.

Today, however, the mother's hunting abilities will not be tested. The time has come for her to pass that challenge on to her offspring. On other sides of the field, Banjo and Swift have positioned themselves, and they are watching the Ornithopods too. Unlike the mother, who is sat down and watching passively, they are both on their feet and tense, judging to see when is the best moment to attack. The Diamantinasaurus' arrival may prove helpful to them. The large and loud herbivore will be a distraction, its presence holding the Ornithopods' attention. Even if this only delays the Ornithopods' reaction time by half a second, that may be all it takes to bring victory to the Australovenators.

Swift looks out on the flock. His hawk-like eyes scan the herd, trying to locate any potential targets. However, targets will only reveal themselves in the chaos and panic that sets in during an attack. The weak, the injured, and the inexperienced can only be detected when they are forced to run. Until then, observing them is pointless. There is no use in prolonging the hunt.

Swift readies himself. Having accompanied and observed his mother on previous hunts, he imitates her usual moves. He bends his legs, lowering his body slowly. He leans forward; shifting his center of balance forward helps with momentum during the run. However, this must be done carefully. If the center of balance is too far forward, turning mid-run will be hard, and may even prove dangerous should Swift be unable to keep his balance.

A deep breath, and Swift charges. He bursts from the shadows. The Ornithopods react almost instantly, getting to their feet and running. Swift scans the flock as he runs. Despite covering a dozen meters every second, the combined forces of his powerful bird-like brain, inner ear, and neurons located throughout his muscles allow him to keep his head steady as he careens along. His eyes flit about rapidly. An Ornithopod stumbles. Perhaps it is wounded? Perhaps it is inexperienced? Whatever the case, Swift realizes his chances of success are highest with this individual.

He turns and gives chase. The Ornithopod is fast too, moving at almost the same speed as Swift.

From the forest, the mother watches. She sees Swift getting closer. She watches as he readies his arms to reach out and deal the determining blow.

Then, in a second, the Ornithopod turns. Swift lashes out, but his claws cut through the air and make no contact. Swift has underestimated his target, and cannot turn as quickly. In danger of losing his balance and breaking a limb, he is forced to slow down and come to a stop. By the time he does so, the Ornithischian is two dozen meters away. Even if Swift were to give chase, the element of surprise is lost, and his energy has been greatly expended.

Suddenly, Banjo bursts in. He dashes past Swift and closes the distance rapidly on the Ornithopod.

Caught by surprise, the Ornithopod turns. However, it has timed its turn too soon, and this only costs it time as Banjo readjusts his course easily, and gains ever closer.

Banjo lashes out, carving a wide arc through the air with his massive claws. One of them connects with the Ornithopod's tail, tearing through the flesh. The Ornithopod stumbles and falls to the ground. Banjo, carried by his momentum, overshoots it. He comes to a stop and turns to face his prey. The Ornithopod gets up rapidly, but not swiftly enough. Banjo hooks both his hands' claws into its sides and throws the Ornithopod back to the ground. He raises his foot and steps on its chest, pinning it to the ground. Then, in one quick move, he leans over and bites down on its neck.

The hunt is over. Banjo picks up his kill in his hands, and he turns and strides off to the forest, where his mother is waiting. Swift walks behind his brother, happy that the hunt was successful, even if he did not manage to see it through. Banjo reaches his mother, and she nuzzles him, rubbing her head along his neck in a sign of familiarity. If Banjo could beam, he would. He has proved himself – for now. Many more tests will be needed to prove that they are ready, but their practice has gotten off to a good start. At the very least, they have a meal to tide them over for the next week.

Chapter 4

One year later. Another clearing, but in a different forest, almost a hundred kilometers away. This one is large, and dotted with lone conifer trees. These provide much-wanted shade from the hot summer sun for several Ornithopods. The mottled green pattern of their feathers makes them blend in with the roots of the trees, but Swift can still manage to see them. Although he cannot make out how many they are, he knows they are there.

A few other Ornithopods nip at the fronds of ferns, clustered around the clearing's edge. They are on their feet, and alert. Swift knows they will scatter the moment he steps out from the trees surrounding the clearing. The Ornithopods lying in the cool shade are his best bet. He focuses on the tree closest to him. At least one Ornithopod can be seen lying there. He steels himself.

The Ornithopods who are standing and grazing react instantly as he bursts from the trees. They flee quickly, but Swift pays them no attention. The Ornithopods in the shade of the trees are slower to react, but they are still on their feet just a few seconds after his charge. They turn and run, slowly at first, to avoid tripping on any tree roots, as that would doom them. Once out of the shade of the tree, they pick up speed.

Swift, however, has already reached top speed, and his long strides carry him ever nearer. Before he can get too close, the Ornithopods turn and scatter, splitting up and running off in different directions. Thinking rapidly, Swift selects a target, an average-sized individual who has run off to the right.

Swift turns to face the Ornithopod as it flees, costing him a second. He then picks up speed again and begins catching up to it. The Ornithopod continues running as fast as it can, heading for the trees. This is a risky move; like Swift, it may trip on the undergrowth. However, it knows no Australovenator will even think of risking a chase in the dense forest. Fueled by adrenaline, it runs onward. However, Swift draws ever closer.

Suddenly, another Ornithopod, confused and disoriented by the chaos, dashes past, several meters in front of Swift. For a moment, Swift is distracted as he considers chasing the speeding animal. However, as the Ornithopod runs off to his right, there is no point considering it. There is no way Swift can make a 90 degree turn while running.

His attention returns to the Ornithopod he was pursuing. However, to Swift's shock, it is no longer there. Glancing to his left, Swift sees it; through dumb luck, it had decided to try and make a break for the left at the very moment Swift was distracted. Already sidetracked by the other Ornithopod that had just run past, Swift staggers and comes to a halt. Tired and out of breath, he can only watch as the Ornithopod runs off.

A few minutes later, and Swift has caught his breath. With the Ornithopods nowhere to be seen, all having fled into the forest, he has no choice but to call it a day. Despondent, he turns and trudges away.

Half an hour later, his defeated march takes him out of the forest and into the open expanse surrounding it. The Australian lands are hotter than they were the year before, and the rains are much less frequent. This is all just part of a multi-year cycle of wet years and dry years, but the animals and plants are starting to feel the change, especially here in the open plains. Shrubs and thorny trees are dotted about as far as the eye can see, and the ground at Swift's feet is red and dusty. But this shrubland, and the forests around it, are what Swift calls home. This is his territory.

At 7 years of age, he is now fully grown, as indicated by a series of white bands of feathers running down the length of his tail. A little under 6 meters long, he is not as large as his mother, but still capable of being a formidable predator.

Unfortunately, he isn't quite there yet. For all Australovenators, most hunts are unsuccessful, but Swift's more than most. Ever since his mother forced him to leave her care and protection several months ago, in order to strike out on his own and establish a territory, he has been struggling. He hasn't made a kill in weeks.

For most Australovenators, this would leave them in a terrible position. Unable to find food, he should be starving, and this, in turn, should make him weaker and less likely to succeed in later hunts. However, he is still healthy and well-fed.

Eventually, Swift reaches his resting spot. A short, 15-meter tall Angiosperm tree, its branches covered in dry leaves, has only just managed to grow in this terrain. Crouching down, Swift sits in the shade beneath its branches, head thrown back, mouth slightly open, panting. Looking out across the horizon, he can see forests in the distance. They, too, form part of his vast territory.

Swift spots something and looks harder. A shape is moving across the shrubland. Approaching. The figure is large, around Swift's size. Ordinarily, Swift would be afraid, or at the very least nervous, but Swift knows this shape.

Several minutes later, and the creature reaches him. In its clawed hands is an Ornithopod, freshly killed. The Ornithopod is dropped in front of Swift. He glances at it for a second and then looks up at his brother.

Getting to his feet, Swift is slightly shorter than Banjo. At over 6 meters long, Banjo has surpassed their mother in size. Fit and skilled, he is a very capable predator. His successful kill rate is a testament to his abilities and physical prowess; almost 40% of his hunts are successes. And this is how Swift has been surviving.

The two brothers nuzzle affectionately. Due to their bond, they decided to form a territory together. They share it as partners. They do not hunt together. Like most meat-eating dinosaurs, Australovenators do not have intelligent pack-hunting coordination, and at best will hunt as a mob, overpowering prey through numbers. Banjo and Swift hunt individually, and share their kills.

Banjo takes a few steps back, leaving Swift standing alone over the Ornithopod. Banjo is letting his brother have first pick. Swift is hesitant; he knows his brother deserves this more, as he is the one who made the kill. Banjo sits down, a sign of refusal. Gratitude filling Swift, he too sits down, and he begins digging into the kill. He cannot bring himself to eat his fill, however, and before long, he gets up again. Lowering his arms, he gently nudges the kill towards Banjo and then retreats into the shade to rest. Tired, he lays his weary head down to rest. The sounds of Banjo eating fade away as he drifts off to sleep.

Eventually, Banjo stops eating. His appetite satiated, he gets to his feet and walks towards his brother. Lying by his side, he rests his head against the head of his younger brother. One might argue that, for Banjo, the logical thing to do would be to strike out on his own, and get his own territory where he does not need to share with his brother. This thought could not be farther from Banjo's mind.

Chapter 5

There is another reason why Banjo and Swift's mother forced them to leave her territory. It is time for them to have their own families. Both are now old enough to find mates who will bear their offspring, and who they may share their own territories with, at least until the offspring are old enough to not require the care of two parents. However, in the vast world of the Australovenators, riddled with the many large territories of other Australovenators, finding a mate is hard. The males cannot leave their territories, as other males will not tolerate their presence in their own territories. They can but wait for a nomadic female, looking for a mate, to wander into their land.

12 days later.

Banjo and Swift lie resting by the carcass of an Ornithopod. Banjo's kill, of course. Flies buzz around it excitedly. A few settle on Banjo's face, crawling over the scales, which are speckled with blood and tiny bits of flesh from the day's feeding.

Suddenly, Banjo perks up and lifts his head, sending the flies scattering. A scent has cut through the stench of the herbivore's corpse. A scent that doesn't bring to mind food, or danger. A scent of familiarity. Another Australovenator.

Swift looks up too, having caught on to the smell. The two get to their feet. Leaving the carcass, they move off through the shrubland, following the scent.

15 minutes later, and they have gotten close. Tentatively, they approach a watering hole, a moderately large pond. Ornithopods and other small dinosaurs are nowhere to be seen. They all fled the water's edge long ago, as they too had picked up the scent of the then-approaching Australovenator, which now drinks from the water. Banjo

and Swift approach and the Australovenator looks up. The two males observe her, scanning her body for an indication as to whether or not she is a threat. Their eyes turn to the tail. Unlike both Banjo and Swift, the white bands of feathers are not present on the tail; it is just covered in an unadorned reddish-brown coat of feathers. The white feathers on Banjo and Swift's tail are a sign of their sexual maturity, and also of their sex, revealing them to be male. This is ingrained deep inside their brains. Recognizing the absence of those feathers on the other Australovenator, they understand that she is a female. Her large size suggests that she is fully grown and ready to mate. The question they need to find the answer to is whether or not she is willing to mate. Her having entered their territory suggests she may be looking for males. However, it is also possible she was forced to flee her territory, and wandered into theirs.

The female, who had been watching them as she drank, now stands up, her thirst quenched. She approaches them slowly, hesitantly. She looks over the two males in front of her. She is only slightly older than they are; she has not had a mate before.

Banjo and Swift approach too. They are just as hesitant, if not more. A wrong move on their part and they might scare her off. In the mating game, female Australovenators get to call the shots and can leave at the slightest discomfort. Banjo and Swift must be gentle and make sure that their intentions are clear.

Instinctively, Banjo and Swift lower their bodies, leaning forward, so that the female stands taller than either of them. This gives her a sense of power and shows their submissiveness to her. She calls out, a light, bird-like warble. Banjo and Swift follow suit. A level of communication is established. Then, in a decisive move, the female lowers her head for a second. She lets out a low rumble. Swift and Banjo's hearts leap; she is interested. This, they know, means the challenge has now changed. They no longer need to worry about making her feel secure and comfortable. Now, they must win her over.

Swift is suddenly hit by a pang of nervousness. The female will only choose one suitor, and the challenge is not as simple as it seems. Winning her over will, for the first time in his life, bring him into direct competition with his brother. But Swift puts that thought from his mind. It is the female's choice; all that Swift needs to concern himself with now is making himself attractive to her.

As Swift contemplates how to present himself, Banjo makes the first move. He leans back, raising his torso and head. Spreading out his arms, he lets out a low call – he is not trying to be threatening, merely imposing. The best way for an Australovenator to make himself appear attractive is to make himself look strong. This is ingrained deep into their minds. It's nothing more than natural selection; females will try to pick the strongest individuals as mates, who will give their offspring the best chance of survival.

Swift then makes his move. He tries to imitate his brother and rears up. However, as he sizes up next to Banjo, his brother comes in at a half-meter taller than him. The female is clearly more impressed with Banjo, and her attention is fixed on him. Proud, Banjo's courage is boosted, and he lets out a slightly louder call. He is beginning to try and assert himself. Swift's self-confidence has taken a hit. However, the female sneaks a few glances in his direction. She is still interested, and she makes eye contact with Swift. Swift isn't out of the running yet, but he will need to try something new. Imitating his brother will not work.

Swift lowers himself, crouching down. Putting all his effort into his tail, he raises it high behind him. He waves it as best he can, showcasing the white bands. He calls out, and his is a long, guttural call. A rumble coming from the back of the throat. He doesn't even need to open his mouth; the vibrations emanate from his throat and deep into the female's bones. It is almost haunting. But it is not a show of strength. And, for that reason, Banjo is almost assured of his success. Swift will have to wait for the next female.

However, the female still isn't biting. She turns, and off she walks. Banjo and Swift call out to her, but she ignores their pleas. They too set off, following her, but keeping a safe distance for fear of unsettling her. They walk away from the watering hole, towards Banjo and Swift's tree. Here, in its shade, the female sits herself down.

Banjo and Swift halt, taken aback. The female is not leaving them. Perhaps, then, there is still hope. Perhaps she is not done testing them. Banjo and Swift watch her, hesitantly, contemplating their next move. She lifts her large, lethal claws and scratches her neck lazily, irritated by the dust and insects. Banjo and Swift approach her, only for her to turn and hiss at them. Backing away, they lie down at a distance from her. Both sets of eyes are trained on her, and she knows it.

Wooing her will take time. But it is time they are both willing to spend.

Late afternoon. The sun is low in the reddening sky. The shadows have grown long, and the dirt of the scrublands is red in the dying light. Banjo is sound asleep in a copse of bushes. Swift is awake, watching primitive birds fly to and from the watering hole. The female, still near the tree, gets up. Shaking some of the dust from her feathers, she starts walking off. Swift notices and gets to his feet. He watches as she heads for the watering hole. Ultimately, his interest in the female gets the better of him, and he follows.

At the watering hole, the female descends for a drink. Swift moves through the trees, keeping an eye on her. He decides to approach her, but not from behind. He circles around until he comes into her line of sight to her left. She glances at him. He stands, unsure as to what to do now that he is alone with her. She raises herself to her full height. She, like Banjo, is bigger than him. Swift stares at her, half daunted, half enraptured. She stares back, though her eyes are judgmental.

In the trees, several primitive birds chirp and call. Vocals not too different from Swift's own. He calls, a light warble. The female does not return it, merely cocking her head to one side. She ignores Swift's attempts at familiarity, leaving Swift clueless as to her intentions.

The birds are silent now. All eyes are on the two Australovenators. Left ignored, Swift's calls die down. The female watches for a few more seconds, taking in every minute detail of Swift's stance and physique. Her assessment concluded, she turns and walks away from him, back to the treeline around the water. Off through the trees and on to the shrubland she goes, leaving Swift standing by the pool, one foot in the water.

Night. A chill descends under the open sky. The Australovenators do not feel it as they sleep, their feathers providing them with more than enough warmth. The moon's light reveals the female under the tree she now calls hers, sleeping soundly. Swift sleeps well too. Banjo is slightly restless, having slept during the day, but he slumbers nonetheless. Fortunately for all, they get their rest. They need it, as the next day is going to be a big one.

Late morning. The sun rises, almost at its highest point in the sky. The female sits upright, looking out over the shrublands. In the distance, a group of Ornithopods traverses timidly. She is silent.

Banjo moves towards her. He calls out to her, and she is silent. He moves closer, and still, she does not react. Swift attentively observes his brother's advances. He does not want to risk his brother wooing her outside his presence.

The female eventually turns to Banjo, looking at him with her head slightly tilted. She is inquisitive. Banjo calls out to her and starts puffing out the feathers on his chest. He is checking to see if she tolerates him and whether she will allow any advances. She does not reprimand him.

Swift rises and moves to them, seeing that the female appears receptive. His brother eyes him suspiciously. They lock eyes as Swift walks up to them. Banjo snaps, hissing slightly. Swift recoils, taken aback by this outburst. Instinctively, he returns it in kind, opening his jaws and hissing back. He stares into his brother's eyes and sees himself reflected in the large black pupils. For a moment, the female is forgotten. All Swift sees is Banjo's emotionless stare and his rigid stance. Swift flexes his claws, the tension brought about by their conflicting desires making him uncomfortable.

From the corner of his eye, he sees the female rise to her feet, interested. She stands and faces them, almost bemused. The two males break their stare and turn towards her. Banjo lets out one last hiss at Swift, who growls, annoyed, and takes a few steps away from his brother, while still making sure he is no farther from the female than Banjo is.

Banjo ruffles his feathers, to increase his size, and spreads out his arms. He trills, a deep, powerful warble. Swift calls out lightly. His song, so to speak, is of a higher, piercing pitch. He too spreads out his arms, but also splays his fingers, to try and compensate for his shorter arm-span.

Banjo stomps the ground with his feet, pounding at the dirt. Swift tries the same, but his weight and strength are not equal to his brother's. Swift decides to try something new, and, with his left foot, claws at the ground, kicking up copious amounts of dust and twigs. The female stares at his foot and the dust, interested.

Banjo then tries one final display of strength, leaping up into the air and then coming down to the ground on both feet. He screeches loudly as he does so. Banjo's display is all about noise and power. As Banjo sees it, his show is a symbol of an Australovenator's greatest strengths.

Swift, having no more material, wraps up his display with a low, mournful call. He then rears up, but is no taller than the female. He does not try to look down on her; instead, he stares straight into her beautiful orange eyes, their big black pupils so full of mystery and intrigue.

She stares at both of them, shifting her gaze between them. Long, studious looks. Banjo and Swift tense up. The eyes of both are locked on the female. Any tension between them has dissipated in the face of the pressure they feel in anticipation of the female's choice.

Then, after what feels to the males like an eternity, the female locks eyes with Banjo. Banjo feels a rush of adrenaline, bolstered by hope. And then, eyes still on Banjo, the female struts assuredly towards Swift.

Banjo watches shocked as she moves towards his smaller, *inferior* brother and rubs her neck against his, glancing at Banjo all the while.

Adrenaline pumps through Swift's body. Surprise racks his brain. Against all expectations, against all the odds, he was chosen.

Banjo screams.

Swift is jolted out of his reverie, and the female glares at Banjo. Swift looks at Banjo, who has planted his feet down firmly and faces his brother.

Banjo calls again. He is issuing a challenge. Banjo's pride has been hit, and his urge to mate will not go ignored. Swift has been called to fight.

Swift is hesitant. He steps back and is unsure as to what pose to adopt. A submissive one would ease with the tension between him and his brother, but he also needs to impress his new mate. As Swift backs away, the female does not, and she is left standing somewhat isolated.

Banjo turns to her. He calls, and this time it is inviting. He is offering himself to her, suggesting that she may have made a mistake and should change her mind now. The female is silent and still, as though considering it. Then, she turns towards Swift, and, for the first time since choosing Swift, firmly and decisively turns her eyes away from Banjo. Banjo is shattered. But he is not defeated.

Rage coursing through him, powering his muscles, he strides towards the female and bites her on the neck. A soft but firm bite, clamping his jaws around her neck, gripping her tightly. He pulls back, tearing her away from Swift. She stumbles and falls to the ground. For a second, Banjo utterly towers over her, dominating her. Now, she locks eyes with him again. Slowly, she rises to her feet, maintaining eye contact throughout. Her every move is calculated.

She turns and looks at Swift. Swift cowers, shocked by his brother's outburst. The female calls out to him, a pleading call, asking her knight in shining armor to protect her. Fighting his brother is the last thing Swift wants to do. For Banjo, filled with anger and pumping with energy, a fight is exactly what is wanted.

Before Swift can react, Banjo charges him. He bites down on Swift's head, down on the roof of his skull. Swift screams, a combination of surprise and pain. Shaking his neck and body, he breaks free. A few steps back are taken, and he shakes his head to try and clear the ringing in his ears.

Banjo screams in Swift's face. Intimidation. A challenge. Banjo is determined, filled with a new, unfamiliar rage towards his brother. Hurt and shock have fused into an ugly hatred within him.

The female calls out to Swift. A cry for help. She wants Swift to try and protect her. She wants Swift to give her the satisfaction of watching a good fight. The ultimate test of strength.

Swift, reading no more into her cries than pleas for her honor to be defended, fixes his posture, and stands firmly.

Seeing the chance for a fight, Banjo takes it and rushes Swift. He rams into Swift with his right shoulder, and Swift staggers back. Raising his right arm, he hits Swift's shoulder with the back of his hand. Pain courses through Swift, and, instinctively, he retaliates. He clamps his jaws around Banjo's neck, near the base. Banjo snarls as Swift's teeth draw blood. Grabbing Swift by the shoulders, he tries to shake him off. In doing so, his hand claws pierce Swift's skin. The sudden pang of pain causes Swift to loosen his grip. Swift decides to move in closer to his brother, raising his hands while doing so. Imitating his brother, Swift grabs Banjo by the shoulders. Suddenly, the two are locked in a bear-hug, grappling with each other, and trying to throw the other to the ground.

As they struggle, the female watches eagerly. Enraptured by the spectacle of Australovenator strength, she observes every one of their moves, not looking away from them for an instant.

Suddenly, Swift stumbles. With his brother's footing unsteady, Banjo pushes his advantage and throws all his weight into Swift and to the side. Without a firm stance, Swift cannot resist, and he is thrown off-balance. His own weight does the rest of the job, pulling him down to the ground in a cloud of dust and debris.

Snarling, he looks up. Banjo stares down at him. The female, from the sidelines, is transfixed with Banjo. Swift's brother turns to her and notices her fascination. He looks back down at his brother, who is gasping for breath, winded by the fall. Banjo turns away dismissively and takes a few steps closer to the female.

Swift looks up at her. At this moment, he is invisible to her. Her attention is entirely on Banjo. Banjo, whose blows still send pain through Swift's body. He pants heavily, frustration building within him. With newfound strength surging from the feelings of betrayal and anger rushing through him, he places his hands down on the ground, pushes down with his arms, and gets to his feet. Without a second thought, he charges, fueled by his pain, and slams into Banjo sideways, with all his force. Caught off-guard, Banjo stumbles and almost falls. He manages to keep his balance but ends up crouched low. Looking up, he finds the female looking down at him.

The female bends down, bringing her face close to Banjo's. Still unnoticed by her, Swift starts to suspect he may be fighting a losing battle. Banjo, ill at ease with being towered over, stands up to his full height. Looking the female in the eyes, his heart is hardened. Turning to Swift, he is resolute in the knowledge that this fight must be won.

Banjo begins pacing around Swift. Swift begins pacing too, agitated. Banjo walks assuredly, almost strutting with confidence. The female watches, curious as to what Banjo's play will be. Swift tenses up, nervous. He emits a low rumble, trying to calm his brother, but his call falls on deaf ears. For during their pacing, Banjo has placed himself exactly where he wants. He stands, leaning back slightly, his chest and front facing Swift's left side. With Swift in profile, this leaves Banjo with the greatest possible surface area as a target.

Banjo jumps, leaping vertically into the air. As he rises, he arches his back and pulls his legs up. This sends his body slowly rotating back, until, at the peak of his leap, his body is fully vertical. The pads of his feet face Swift's exposed left side.

And he kicks out.

His feet connect loudly with Swift's body, and Swift is flung back. Winded, and with at least one rib broken from the impact, controlling his fall is far from his mind, and Swift comes crashing down to the ground.

Banjo adjusts his position in the air and lands on his feet. He staggers a bit and needs to readjust his footing to keep his balance, but he has remained standing, while Swift lies utterly defeated before him.

The female, her decision made, approaches Banjo. She rubs her neck against his, their feathers ruffling against each other. Banjo turns to face his downed brother, as the female continues rubbing herself over her new mate, claiming him as hers.

Swift, still gasping for air, raises his head. Banjo casts him a glance, but it is just a quick one, and he looks away quickly. Swift screams, or at least tries to. The air knocked out from his lungs, all he can manage is a raspy breath.

Swift gets to his feet, more than a little shakily. The female, draped over Banjo's back as she intertwines their scents, looks at Swift. She hisses, a long, guttural, menacing hiss, before nipping at Banjo's neck. Banjo, knowing what must be done now, opens his mouth and lets out a loud, decisive snarl. Deep and powerful, he advances towards Swift, who backs off. Swift calls out to both of them, and this time he is pleading. Pleading for them to tolerate him, pleading for them to let him remain.

However, he knows they will never tolerate him. Banjo and his mate will need these lands to start their own family, and, once the female begins to bear offspring, they will become extremely aggressive towards any potential threats. The female may very well kill him if he stays. That is the way of all predators. But for Swift, who has relied on his brother's help to survive, leaving his family and their territory and going out to survive and forge his own home will be the greatest challenge of his life.

For now though, Swift has only one thing to do. Run. And he runs, away from his brother and across the dusty shrubland. He runs through the day, until the sun sets. Through the next day, as the sun rises and falls. And on into the night. Swift runs.

Banjo and Swift

Banjo and Swift

Part One: The Science

Near the town of Winton, in Queensland, is a plot of pasture land – grazing land for cattle – known as Elderslie Station. In 2005, the owner made a discovery that would put the Winton are in the spotlight for Australian paleontology forever – the bones of a dinosaur. The Australian Age of Dinosaurs Museum of Natural History began excavating the site in 2006, and it was soon found that the bones belonged to a large Titanosaur, a herbivorous dinosaur, which was nicknamed Matilda. Several years later, it would come to be formally named *Diamantinasaurus matildae*.

As excavations continued, more bones turned up. It soon became apparent that bones from another dinosaur were preserved at the site. In 2008, when enough of the bones were removed from the ground, the team realized they had discovered the bones of a predatory dinosaur new to science. One year later, when the remains had been properly studied, they named it *Australovenator wintonensis* – the Southern Hunter from Winton.

Australovenator was a sight to behold – stretching a bit under 6 meters in length, and nearly 2 meters tall at its back, this specimen was Australia's largest predatory dinosaur known at the time. It was also its best-preserved – almost 30% of the original skeleton was found, and as the years went on even more bones were unearthed.

The most remarkable feature of Australovenator is its hand. It has three fingers, with the first two fingers bearing huge, curved claws. However, it is more complex than that. Firstly, although similar in size, the two large claws are different in shape. The first claw is thin, and blade-like, while the second claw is thick, like a hook. The reason for this is still not known, but it is a feature present in both Australovenator and its close relatives.

Its hand is also one of the most advanced and complex hands of any dinosaur. Its fingers were hyperextensible, meaning the joints could expand and loosen, making the fingers almost extend. This feature suggests its hands played a significant role in hunting, helping it kill its prey. However, its fingers were also extremely flexible, which suggests it used its hands to help it eat, picking up its food to bring it to its mouth. Even its arm was very mobile – Australovenator could stretch and swing its arms with ease, helping it draw food closer to its mouth and chest.

The next highly advanced feature of Australovenator is its legs. Its legs were huge for its size, far taller proportionally than most other large theropod dinosaurs. This shows it was fast – very fast. It has even been called "the cheetah of the Cretaceous" due to the impressive speed it would have had. However, speed is not the only power its legs had.

In the confrontation between Swift and Banjo, Banjo ultimately defeats Swift by leaping up and kicking him. This is a move used by another Australian dinosaur, one which is alive today: the Cassowary, a very large flightless bird, which will jump up and kick out in self-defense. The reason for giving Banjo the ability to do this in the story is based on the results of a 2016 study of the preserved foot bones of Australovenator. Firstly, the claw of Australovenator's inner toe (the equivalent of a human big toe) is the longest of Australovenator's toe-claws. This automatically draws a comparison with the Cassowary, which also has its longest claw on its inner toe. This is to help the Cassowary inflict as much damage as possible; when kicking out, the large inner claw delivers a deep cut to its opponent. Additionally, Australovenator's inner toe claw is damaged and bruised, and the scientists who studied it suspect that the bruising might have been caused by repeated impacts with the claw, such as those caused by kicking. Overall, this suggests Australovenator is the only extinct dinosaur for which direct evidence of this deadly ability has been found.

Lastly, there is Australovenator's skull. The skull of Australovenator is not as well preserved as its arms and legs, but a large part of its lower jaw was found. Its lower jaw was not exceptionally long or powerful – this was not its primary weapon. Although the sharp, serrated teeth would have definitely been able to inflict damage, it is likelier that it used its arms to take down prey, and then used its jaws for the finishing touch.

Which leaves the question of what Australovenator hunted. At first, the evidence might seem to suggest Australovenator ate large sauropods, like Diamantinasaurus. As already said, the only known skeleton of Australovenator was found together with a Diamantinasaurus, and furthermore sauropod bones found elsewhere in the Winton are often found together with Australovenator teeth. However, in reality all that this shows is Australovenator probably ate large sauropods. There is no evidence to suggest it actually killed them – it may have just been eating them after they had died, either of old age or some illness.

Indeed, Australovenator's morphology (its body shape and physique) suggests a different kind of prey. Australovenator is very lightly built, and its long legs suggest it hunted fast prey, unlike the large and slow-moving sauropods. Australovenator's hands and claws suggest it slashed and grabbed prey, and this technique would work best on animals smaller than itself. And the Winton Formation preserves evidence of small-bodied dinosaurs, which could be potential prey for Australovenator. Several skeletons of a small Ornithopod dinosaur, a two-legged herbivorous dinosaur, were found in the Winton Formation during the late 2010s. Although these animals would have lived 5 million years before *Australovenator wintonensis*, they show that Ornithopods had long been present in the formation, and fossilized footprints confirm that they were still present during Australovenator's time.

In the story, the Australovenators are portrayed as being covered in feathers. As with most prehistoric dinosaurs, there is no direct evidence showing whether or not they had feathers. Therefore, to try and get a good idea of what is most likely, it is common to look at the evidence known among related species of dinosaurs, as well as other factors.

Australovenator is known to be a type of Megaraptoran, which is a group of large, lightly-built two-legged dinosaurs known from Asia, South America, and Australia. Unfortunately, there is no direct evidence for whether Megaraptorans had feathers and/or scales, so their relatives must be considered. There is still a lot of debate among scientists as to what type of meat-eating dinosaurs Megaraptorans are related to, but the weight of evidence currently suggests they are coelurosaurs, which is a line of dinosaurs that contains both *Tyrannosaurus rex*, the dromaeosaurs (the family including Velociraptor), and modern birds.

Fortunately, there is a lot of evidence indicating what different coelurosaurs had as skin covering. For almost all of them, there is evidence that they had a lot of feathers. The only exceptions are *T. rex* and its very large and very close relatives, who presumably lost most of their feathers due to the warm environments they lived in and their massive size (like how Elephants have much less hair than Mammoths). Looking back at Megaraptorans and Australovenator, although they were large animals they were still much less heavily built animals than large Tyrannosaurs. Moreover, the environment of the Winton Formation was occasionally subject to much cooler temperatures than *T. rex* would have encountered. Therefore, it seems reasonable to assume Australovenator was at least partly covered in feathers.

Overall, thanks to the excellent amount of skeletal material preserved for Australovenator, and the evidence we have from its relatives, a very clear picture of what this dinosaur would look and act like has emerged. But what about the other animals of the Winton Formation, the creatures Australovenator would have shared its environment with?

First off, there is Diamantinasaurus. It is a Titanosaur dinosaur, Titanosaurs being a group of sauropod dinosaurs which, like the Megaraptorans, were most common in South America. In addition to the first specimen, which was found together with the Australovenator skeleton, multiple new specimens have been discovered since, making it the best-preserved dinosaur from the Winton Formation. It was not the only Titanosaur in the Winton Formation, which was also home to close relatives of Diamantinasaurus, such as the slightly smaller Wintonotitan, the recently described and even larger Australotitan, and another sauropod which will be appearing in the story soon…

Then there are the Ornithopods. As mentioned earlier, small Ornithopods were present in the Winton Formation before Australovenator lived, and footprints show they were also present at the same time as Australovenator. These would have been small two-legged herbivorous dinosaurs, with a long tail and a jaw which had both teeth and a short beak at the tip.

In the story, the Ornithopods are shown having a coat of feathers. This is because Ornithopods are a type of Neornithischian, and a species of Neornithischian has been found with feathers. Discovered in Russia, and given the name Kulindadromeus in 2014, the fossils of this species showed evidence of long hair-like filaments. It is likely, therefore, that these filaments, thought by some scientists to be similar to the feathers of theropod dinosaurs (a group which includes Australovenator and birds), would also be present on all small Neornithischians, including the Ornithopods in the Winton Formation. It is important to note, however, that not all scientists agree that these filaments are really feathers. It is possible that they merely share a common ancestry with feathers and are not true feathers. However, for the sake of simplicity, they were referred to as "feathers" in this story.

Lastly, Isisfordia is another resident of the Winton Formation portrayed in this book. Isisfordia is a very well-preserved crocodilian known from multiple parts of Australia, and the species from the

Winton Formation (*Isisfordia duncani*) is known from multiple specimens. A crocodyliform closely related to the ancestors of modern crocodiles, it would have been around one meter in length. With an armored body and a long, wide snout, it would have looked very similar to the crocodiles of today. Like the modern-day Freshwater Crocodile of Australia, it would probably have been an opportunistic predator, attacking anything it could eat, from fish to lizards and even birds if it got the chance.

The animals of the Winton Formation are extremely well-documented, with many insects, mammals, and reptiles also known from the region. Moreover, the flora (plant-life) and even the weather in the Winton Formation 95 million years ago are well-known and allow for a detailed reconstruction of this ancient environment. However, that is something that will be discussed later. Now, it is time to return to Swift's story…

Banjo and Swift

Part Two

Banjo and Swift

Chapter 1

The water heaves back and forth. The sand darkens and lightens as it wettens and dries with each ebb and flow of the lapping waves. Further out to sea, the surface glistens with the dazzling reflections of the midday sun. Creatures fly above the waves – not birds, but large winged reptiles. Beneath the sea, massive, deadly creatures swim, their muscular bodies rippling with momentum.

A forest. Thick, and made up of everything from pines to ginkgo trees, and early flowering trees to cycads. Their leaves are wet, and the ground is soft. The melody of creeks flowing along weaves through the trees. Squawks and flutters of bird-like creatures, hopping and trotting on the forest floor, permeate the thick, steamy air. In the distance, lumbering giants call out to each other as they munch on the lush vegetation.

Deep within the forest, a creature new to this place stalks through the cover of the trees. Two tall legs. Large, powerful arms. A feathered coat. After days of walking, Swift has left the open plains and scattered forests of his brother's territory far behind him, and has found himself in an all-new world. Fortunately for him, he has not detected any sign that another Australovenator is present. However, he has also not seen very much in the way of any large life at all. No Ornithopods, nothing larger than the average bird. He has heard the inhabitants, flitting through the forest, chattering with each other, or just to themselves. Even then, nothing loud, only the occasional rustling of fern leaves and high-pitched calls. Hopefully, the lack of an Australovenator's presence here does not have to do with a lack of food sources.

However, for Swift there is a more pressing crisis. He has not drunk in days and needs to find water soon. Fortunately, the song of running water reaches his ears quickly. Following it, he stumbles across a welcome sight. A creek, its surface clear and sparkling, runs through the forest. Lowering his head, he lets his lower jaw hang down, and the cool water flows into his mouth. Eager to quench his thirst, he gulps it down.

Suddenly, there is a rustling in the ferns nearby. Swift looks up, alert. His eyes flit from tree to tree, looking for a sign of movement. A fern shakes, and something skitters away, but he does not turn quickly enough and cannot get a good glimpse. Something is there, however. That much is sure. Swift waits. Standing as still as possible, he turns his head slowly, scanning the forest.

Another rustling, and he turns his head to the right to look for the source. Just then, a second rustling, this time to his left. Too far apart to be the same creature. There must be more than one of them. Swift sniffs the air. He can certainly smell something, possibly numerous animals, but the scent is unfamiliar. This is new.

Swift decides to wait longer, but as the minutes tick by, nothing happens. No sound, no creatures. Nothing. Eventually, he gets bored. There is still more exploring to be done. Surely there is some larger life here, some other large dinosaurs.

And so he turns away and ambles off through the trees. Bearing in mind where the creek is, should he need to return, he walks on through the forest, aimlessly. On and on he walks, hearing sounds and chittering throughout the forest, as small creatures run under the cover of ferns and low-growing plants, but never seeing anything.

And then he sees a clearing. Sunlight, bright and unfiltered by trees and the forest canopy. An open plain, perhaps? But there is a new sound. A gentle sound, like the rustling of leaves but larger. More constant. Without a breeze. As he approaches, he realizes it is more rhythmic than anything he has heard before.

And then he steps out of the forest and, for the first time in his life, he finds himself looking at a beach.

Sprawled out in front of him, beyond the broad strip of white and beige sand and beneath a cloudless sky, is an endless azure blue. Dappled with flashes of sparkling white, and bringing with it wonderful new smells and sounds is the sea. A quiet wind means the lapping is gentle, and the waves are low. The smell of salt flows to Swift's nostrils. He listens attentively to the beauty of the flow of this massive being, teaming and brimming with countless hidden lives, all intertwined in a chaotic battle of love and survival that Swift cannot even begin to imagine, let alone comprehend.

Intrigued, Swift steps forward. His foot lands on the sand, and the grains stick themselves on his foot. He takes another step and begins to slide on the loose sand. He stops, uneasy about his balance. Before he can readjust himself, his feet start to sink. He pulls his feet from the sand and widens his stance, splaying he toes. Eventually, he reaches some degree of comfort in his stability, and presses onward.

His foot makes contact with the water as the waves lap the shoreline. Cool and wet, the feeling is at least a familiar one. This is nothing more than water, just in quantity the likes of which Swift has never encountered before. He hunkers down and lowers his head to the surface. Surely if this feels like water, it must be ordinary water? There is something in the smell that is different, however, and Swift is hesitant. Eventually, the knowledge that such an amount of potentially drinkable water lies before him is too much to resist, and he opens his mouth and takes a drink. Instantly, he retches, coughing up the saline water. The taste is disgusting and serves as a warning that this water will not suffice as a means to satisfy his thirst. He will need to return to the creek the next time he needs to drink.

Still shaking his head from the disgusting taste, he looks up as he hears a vaguely familiar sound. Loud calls, which must be from large creatures. Bellows, which recall an acquaintance. As he turns to face the origin of the calls, he finds himself looking at a group of massive dinosaurs.

These are Savannasaurus. Very close relatives of the gigantic Diamantinasaurus, these beasts are a sight to behold. Like the Diamantinasaurus, they are 15 meters long and sport long necks and tails, small heads, and tall columnar legs. However, these titanosaurs are even larger than the Diamantinasaurus in total size, as their torsos are almost twice as wide as the Diamantinasaurus', and their legs are longer and more robust as a result of the extra weight.

As the trio of titanic dinosaurs approaches Swift, their feet sink into the sand. These dinosaurs, like Diamantinasaurus, do not have splayed toes. Instead, their feet are more like columns and bring to mind elephant feet rather than bird feet. As a result, they do not have a large surface area and cannot stay on top of the sandy beach like the Australovenator's feet can. This means they cannot move particularly quickly. However, when you are practically immune from harm, what's the rush? These sauropods have lived here on the beaches without encountering any large predators in years. Even an Australovenator, the largest meat-eating dinosaur in these lands, is no match for an adult Savannasaurus. More than twice as long, and weighing over 20 times as much, the sheer weight and volume of a Savannasaurus is protection enough. And they're no walking lumps of meat either; their long tail can be a deadly weapon, with the potential to kill an adult Australovenator with a single swing. And their backs are covered in a double row of defensive osteoderms – conical pieces of bone on top of the skin. Swift wanted large dinosaurs, but this is more than he bargained for. Still, it must be comforting to know that these dinosaurs are here. Wherever giants are, a thriving ecosystem, including smaller, more manageable prey, is likely to be found.

A few minutes later, the Savannasaurus turn away from Swift and trundle off to the trees on the side of the beach. Raising their necks, they bury their heads in the branches of the trees and begin plucking off leaves. Swift observes them, but a new sound grabs his attention.

A loud cawing noise emanates from the sea. Looking out over the water, Swift spies a pair of the flying reptiles squabbling with each other. They quarrel over the surface of the water, the downstrokes of their wings keeping them aloft. The dispute is quickly settled, and one of the two flies away, while the other drops to the surface of the water. There, it floats, using its large wings to stay on top of the water's surface.

These are Ferrodraco, and they are a type of flying reptile called pterosaurs. Dinosaurs and pterosaurs are very close relatives, closer to each other than to any other group of animals, but pterosaurs are not dinosaurs. Like many dinosaurs, their bodies are covered in a structure that resembles feathers. However, these are not true feathers like those of the dinosaurs. They are pycnofibres, a type of fuzzy integument closely related to dinosaur feathers.

Pterosaurs like Ferrodraco have wings that are unique in the animal kingdom. Their arms are fairly normal in anatomy, almost similar to a human's arms, except with one difference. The last of their four fingers is extremely long – twice as long as the entire arm. From the tip of this finger all the way down to their knees stretches a large flap of skin, forming the surface of the wing. This membrane is more than just simple skin; it is riddled with nerves and sensors, allowing for precise adjustments mid-flight. This is a highly sophisticated form of flying and is one of the reasons pterosaurs reach sizes birds will never attain. These Ferrodraco are large, with a 4-meter wingspan. However, in the later times of the age of the dinosaurs, pterosaurs will get much bigger, with wingspans of up to 12 meters.

The other Ferrodraco lands on the beach and Swift approaches it. On land, Ferrodraco stand on all fours. They fold their long fourth finger back and walk on their hands and feet. Although this may sound ungainly, advanced pterosaurs like Ferrodraco are actually quite adept on the ground and able to move around with ease.

Ferrodraco's large head is a feature shared by many pterosaurs. Its jaw is long and lined with dozens of thin and needle-like teeth, perfect for catching fish. At the tip of its snout, there is a tall crest, on both the upper and lower sides of its jaws. This is for display purposes; males have larger crests than females, and crest size is a factor when selecting a mate. A larger crest implies a healthier male, and thus a better choice for a female who is looking for companionship.

As Swift approaches the Ferrodraco, it becomes spooked. It backs away from him cautiously, and then turns and launches itself into the air, pushing itself off the ground with its long arms. A few heavy flaps of its wings help the Ferrodraco on its way, and in just a few seconds, it is already flying out across the sea. Swift can do nothing but watch. Suddenly, he hears a commotion. The other Ferrodraco, who was floating on the water's surface, has panicked and taken off from the water's surface in a couple of downstrokes. As it flies away, Swift looks at the rippling, frothing water where the Ferrodraco had been floating. Deep below it, a leviathan swims along. Armed with jaws that are 2 meters long and lined with teeth that can be up to 10 centimeters long, this is a massive predator. The largest predator Australia has ever seen.

But for now, all Swift can do is stare at the idyllic surface of the water. He has no idea of the monsters that lurk in its depths. That will soon change.

Chapter 2

Swift lies down. Hidden among the ferns, his brown feathers slightly blend him in with the forest floor and the bark of the trees. In front of him is the creek. More specifically, its widest point. Swift knows from experience that the largest body of drinkable water is the best place to find prey. All animals need to drink. All Swift has to do is wait.

The shadows crawl across the forest and over his body as the sun makes its way across the big pale blue above. Under the shade of the forest canopy, it is nice and cool. A pleasant change from the hotter forests of his former territory. Calm and relaxed, with nothing to do but wait, Swift finds himself getting drowsy. His eyelids grow heavy, and he gives in and closes his eyes.

He is awoken by a rustling in the ferns and undergrowth. A familiar sound. These must be the same creatures he encountered earlier. He is aware that they are probably watching him. However, he can but hope that they will show themselves eventually and come to drink. Now, he must be vigilant. He wants to see what he is up against; he will not risk missing them.

Another rustle. Another crack of twigs underfoot. A squawk and a chirp. Silence. Something sprints lightly. Silence. Two quick calls. An argument, perhaps. Silence. And then, from the cover of the low-lying plants, a small dinosaur steps out.

Only a meter in length, this is smaller than an Ornithopod and much more lightly built. It is covered from head to toe in large, well-developed feathers, far more advanced than Swift's downy covering. The arms, although similar in structure to Swift's, with three clawed fingers, seem to be more like wings. Long feathers extend from the underside of the arm, and even from the underside of the middle finger, meaning only the first finger is visible. A fan of long bird-like feathers also extends around the tip of the tail. This is probably for display between individuals, possibly to make them appear bigger and intimidate other rivals. Its feet have three toes. The innermost toe has a long, highly curved claw, the use of which is unclear. It may be inherited from ancestors who used it to climb. Alternatively, it may help it kill its prey, for this is a meat-eater, and although its diet consists of small lizards and insects, this diminutive animal is, in fact, the largest carnivorous dinosaur in these forests.

It belongs to an evolutionary group of dinosaurs called Unenlagiines. And it is not alone. A couple more step out from the trees. They approach the water's edge almost warily. Ordinarily, they'd have nothing to fear in these lands, but their small size makes them cautious by nature. The smell of Swift, which has pervaded the forest ever since his arrival, has made them skittish. They drink hurriedly, as Swift watches them.

They are small. Fast, but not dangerous. A potential meal. Swift considers it, his stomach rumbling. Once they finish drinking, the window of opportunity will be gone.

Eventually, Swift comes to the conclusion that he has little to lose and rears up. The Unenlagiines back off, scared. He walks towards them, looking down at them from the other side of the river. They back away, keeping their distance. Then, before he has a chance to attack them, they scatter, running off in different directions. In a matter of seconds, Swift is left standing alone by the creek. He worries; perhaps he will not get another chance to get this close.

Swift drinks from the creek, before heading on his way. He follows the creek downstream and comes out at the beach once again. In the distance, a group of Savannasaurus browses. Swift studies them. Perhaps he will need to resort to hunting them someday. But no, that would be an impossible feat. Should it come to that, he might be forced to leave. A Savannasaurus hunt would be suicidal.

Turning to his right, he sees a group of Ferrodraco, three of them, squabbling over something. He decides to investigate. Getting closer, he sees that they are fighting over a huge fish, which one of them presumably caught. Pycnofibres fly as they peck at each other, their long teeth scratching each other. Swift's stomach gurgles. He does not have a taste for fish, having never eaten it before, but he has nothing left to lose. He charges them, letting out a loud roar. They take to the air in surprise. However, before he can reach them, they land back down, and for a moment, they are united against him. He reaches them and lashes out, snapping his jaws. They recoil, but they recover quickly, clacking their toothy jaws at him. He swipes at one of them. His first swing misses, but his second grazes the snout of one of them, dislodging a tooth. In pain, it shrieks and falls back. Swift then barges towards the other two, and they are forced to fly back to avoid getting trod over. If their wings were to get torn, it could be disastrous.

Swift now finds himself standing over the fish, as the Ferrodraco circle around him. They are annoyingly persistent, and Swift roars, partly in an attempt to scare them off, partly out of frustration. Reaching down, he picks the fish up, almost cradling it in his hands. He then lowers his jaw and takes a bit bite, tearing off the upper third of the fish, and swallowing it whole. Their spirits dampened, the Ferrodraco begin to fall back. Swift, tired of this, walks off, carrying the fish in his hands.

As he walks, he nibbles on the fish, swallowing chunks of flesh and bone. To a hungry Australovenator, it is delicious. But it will not keep him full for long. A few moments later, he has gulped down the whole fish. Behind him, the Ferrodraco take off, flying out to sea. He watches them fly over the surface of the water. One of them flies down and dives into the water. Swift looks, searching for it. Some seconds later it bursts out of the water. It continues flying along and then repeats this. Swift has no way of knowing that the Ferrodraco are fishing, but his brain is beginning to make connections. The Ferrodraco must be hungry. Perhaps they are looking for food?

Ultimately, it is his hunger, and his curiosity, which drives him forward as he begins to walk into the sea. Step after step, through the frothy shallows. He looks down but sees no life. A few small fish, each smaller than one of his claws. Nothing of consequence. So onwards he goes, marching and marching, deeper into the deep blue. Closer and closer to a starving leviathan, waiting just below the water's surface.

Chapter 3

A fish. Long, and thin. Silver scales run down its body. As it flits about the surface, the sun's rays, piercing through the water, send its body sparkling. With strokes of its powerful tail, it moves along calmly.

Suddenly, it senses something in the water. Swimming about, it sees two large columns rising from the sea floor. Something new. Alien. The fish flits about, curious but wary. Strange, frond-like objects cover the columns, floating in the water. The fish circles them, and suddenly finds itself in a shadow. Spooked, it swims off hurriedly.

If the fish had thought to look up, it would have seen a massive silhouette, towering over the water. Swift watches as the fish swims off. His caution meant he merely observed it, as opposed to attempting to catch it. That, and inexperience. Swift has absolutely no clue how to go about actually catching a fish. Time for trial and error.

He decides to approach catching a fish like he would catching an Ornithopod. Claws are the key player; jaws only come in when the chase is almost over. He stretches his fingers, baring his claws, and lowers them close to the water's surface. Another fish, equally large and beautiful, swims towards him. He waits, hoping that it will get within range. Slowly, trying not to betray his presence, he turns his body so that his arms are as close to the fish. Then, once it is within striking distance, he lashes out. A complete miss, the fish flees unharmed. This will take more time than he thought.

And so, Swift waits. Until the next fish comes along. He underestimates its speed, and it dodges his strike and escapes. More waiting. The water grows warmer as the day goes on and on. In the distance, he can see Ferrodraco diving into the water. One of them comes up with a fish, and others flock around it, trying to pester it into giving the fish up. A chaotic dance ensues in mid-air, with the winged beasts maneuvering with grace and finesse that nears that of the large birds that the future holds. Eventually, the Ferrodraco holding the fish in its jaws manages to work it down its jaw and into its neck while in the air. Sensing that they will not get the fish now, the others return to trying to hunt for themselves.

Momentarily distracted, Swift looks back down. Another fish weaves its way around him. He readies himself, preparing for the decisive blow. Just like with Ornithopods, speed is key. However, the precision required here is off the charts. Baring his claws, he waits, hand hovering over the fish. And he strikes. Direct contact! However, the flesh of the fish is soft, and his claws just aren't hook-like enough to embed themselves in it. Instead, his claws go straight through, slicing three great wounds in the side of the fish but failing to actually grab it. The wounded animal swims off rapidly. The injury may, in time, prove fatal, as it will make it an easier target. However, all that is of no importance to Swift. All that matters is that he will not be the one to eat that fish. His attempt failed, and he will need a new tactic.

The jaw, then. Perhaps Swift's teeth will be able to latch on to the fish. He lowers his neck until his jaws hover just above the water. And lower, until the tip of his snout, breaks the surface. Still lower, until– he snorts loudly. A wave washes water up his nose, and he repeatedly sneezes to get it out. Too low. He returns to his previous pose, with his mouth just above the water. The crests of the waves reach his lower jaw, and the salty water wets his teeth.

A fish swims into view. Swift watches it with his eyes, but, because his head is so close to the water, he has a poor view of what is going on below the surface. The fish disappears from sight. He pulls back slightly, lifting his head and scanning the water. There! It pops into view. He turns his body slightly. His head rests above a spot in the water near it. If it can just swim into position…

The fish swims close. Almost right in place. Now or never. Swift lunges, and, to his surprise, he feels his jaws sink into the cold flesh. Pulling back quickly, he feels the fish thrash about in his mouth. He has done it. He has caught the fish. But there is a problem. As long as the fish is in his mouth, he cannot kill it. Loosening his grip to bite down would free the fish, and the fish is still alive and thrashing. Swift has not thought it through.

But this is where the incredible arms and hands of an Australovenator come into play. Lowering his head and extending his arm, hand, and fingers, Swift can reach up and perfectly grab the fish from his jaws. Letting go with his jaws, he has smoothly transferred the fish from his mouth to his hands, and now, with his mouth free, he can reach down and bite the fish's head clean off. The hunt is done; Swift has made a successful kill. A whole new kind of food, and a successful means of predation. Perhaps this could be the key to Swift's survival?

The water explodes. A few meters in front of Swift, the blue water turns white as a massive object breaches the surface. Two meters in length, this is a massive pair of jaws. Swift leaps backward instinctively as the colossal maw opens up, showcasing dozens of enormous teeth that glint in the sunlight. The spray hits Swift as he flies back, losing his balance and splashing down in the water. The sharp teeth just miss him as the jaws snap shut with incredible speed. The huge head comes crashing down to the water, in a splash that engulfs Swift.

Swift gets to his feet rapidly and tries to scramble away. His balance lost, and unable to get a good grip on the soft sand of the seafloor, he half runs and half swims away as the giant jaws snap again, wildly. They miss, and this time it is by a better margin than the first time. As Swift continues to back away, the jaws do not come any closer. The leviathan that these jaws belong to turns and slinks back into the depths of the sea. As Swift stands up and looks out, all he can see is a massive shape, far longer and broader than he is, move away. In a few seconds, all that remain are ripples on the surface. A few seconds more and the water's surface is still. Swift's beating heart is all that indicates it happened at all. That, and the fact that he no longer has his fish, dropped in the chaos.

Retrieving it is far from Swift's mind. He turns and trudges back to the beach. Fishing is no longer an option.

Chapter 4

One day later. By the beach, the Savannasaurus browse as usual, in small groups. On the sand, several Ferrodraco rest. They are not social creatures, and they keep their distance from each other. An inquisitive young Savannasaurus, only 8 meters in length, approaches one of them. The Ferrodraco eyes it cautiously. When it gets too close, the Ferrodraco decides it has had enough, crying out and shaking itself in a threat display. Perturbed, the young titanosaur backs off and returns to browse with the others. Calming down, the Ferrodraco resumes its rest.

The creek glistens as the sun pierces the forest canopy. A light breeze ruffles the forest leaves. This is good. A breeze means scent only travels in one direction. Swift will need this today. He approaches the creek but finds himself upwind. He needs to be downwind of the creek; that way, the breeze will carry his scent away from the creek, and the scent of animals on the banks will be brought to him.

He crosses the creek tentatively. The bottom of the creek is not pebbly or rough, but soft and smooth, and Swift is relieved. Rugged terrain is dangerous for an Australovenator. A broken leg bone due to a fall, or even just a sprain from a misstep, could be disastrous.

Crossing to the other side, he walks on into the cover of the trees. When he feels he is at a safe distance, he stops and lowers himself. Hiding among the ferns, and blanketed by the trees' shadow, he will, once again, wait. Wait for the creek to come alive.

His stomach rumbles. Yesterday's fish has not held him, and he will need to eat again. Impatience boils in him like a fever, but he forces himself to be calm. He has no other option. A rash move would cost him the element of surprise. He must be patient and still. He closes his eyes but does not sleep. Instead, he focuses on his other senses.

In a nearby tree, a bird chirps. It is calling, looking for a mate. In other parts of the forest, there are females, also looking for companionship. The eternal game of life. The ultimate goal for all the creatures of this world. Reproduction. The legacy of offspring. For Swift, the quest for a mate will come to challenge him soon. But for now, that particular challenge is not on his mind. Right now, staying alive is challenge enough . And the ever-present sounds from his stomach are a reminder of this.

Swift sniffs. There is no scent on the wind. Nothing strong. The smell of Unenlagiines lingers, and of wet plants and the summer breeze, but nothing of interest. No fresh animal smell. No scent of meat, either. Having only eaten fish recently, the smell of warm meat, waiting to be eaten and satiate a hungry carnivore is one that he longs for.

Suddenly, a scent. Unenlagiines. Not an old smell from earlier in the day, but a fresh one. Priming his ears, he hears a faint rustling. The tell-tale sign of the feathered creatures.

By the creek, an Unenlagiine emerges. It ruffles its feathers and looks around. No smell, and nothing to be seen. The old confidence that it had before Swift's arrival returns, and it saunters down to the creek. From the trees, several others watch. Deeming it to be safe, they emerge too.

Swift raises his head from where it is lying in the fern fronds. He looks up at the creek. His well-developed eyes focus on the Unenlagiines there. An issue becomes apparent. So far, all the Unenlagiines have gathered on the opposite side of the creek. He knows the riverbed is safe to walk and even run on, but he would still prefer not to risk it.

Then, an Unenlagiine comes into view. This one is on his side of the creek. She is smaller, and her feathers are not as bright. A female. One of the males on the other bank approaches the creek's edge, contemplating crossing over. The Unenlagiines are the opposite of the Ferrodraco, and take pleasure in each other's company during times of leisure.

The male Unenlagiine begins walking into the creek, then stops. Unenlagiine legs are thin and spindly. Like with Swift, a damaged bone could be catastrophic. However, the Unenlagiine decides to take the risk, and nimbly runs across. Then, its feet hit dry ground; it has made it across safely. It chirps at the female— a form of greeting. The two acknowledge each other's presence, and then the female drinks.

Another Unenlagiine decides to cross over, running across with its wing-like arms spread out for balance. Three Unenlagiines are now on the same bank as Swift. His chances now are reasonably decent. Might as well go for it.

He stands up, still hidden in the shade of the trees. He steps out of the ferns and establishes a secure footing on the forest floor. He watches, eagerly, waiting for them to be the most at ease, so that they are slowest to react. Several have lowered their heads to drink. Perhaps now…

Suddenly, two of the Unenlagiines in the back start squabbling. A light, playful squabble, more for practice than actual confrontation. Nonetheless, it attracts attention, and several of the dinosaurs perk up and turn to watch the commotion. Their attention captivated, Swift decides to make his move.

The quarreling Unenlagiines chirp and twitter, nipping at each other. A few feathers fly. Just then, a crashing underfoot is heard from the other side of the forest. The Unenlagiines around them turn, just in time to see Swift burst into the small clearing around the creek.

The three Unenlagiines on his side of the creek scatter quickly. Swift lashes out, but his jaws miss the fast and agile creatures, which accelerated quickly. His momentum still with him, Swift decides to run across to the other side, splashing through the water, and churning the crystal clear creek into a slush of brown silt. The squabbling Unenlagiines turn and run into the forest, weaving through the trees and over fallen branches.

Three of the Unenlagiines turn and run along the creek, preferring to try their luck in a straight race along the open sides of the stream. Swift stops and turns, watching them run off. He then gives chase. The ground beneath his feet is uneven and littered with twigs and stones. Rather than run, he paces along carefully. Nonetheless, his stride length compensates for his slower speed compared to the Unenlagiines.

As they near the beach, one of the three peels off from the rest, turning to dash into the forest. Swift turns to try and grab it. He opens his mouth wide and lashes out, but his jaws close on thin air. His momentum lost, Swift turns to try and catch up to the others. However, he has lost ground, and all he can do is follow them.

The Unenlagiines run out on to the beach. On the soft sand, they slow down. Swift strides out of the forest behind them. They back away. Much lighter, they do not run the risk of having their feet sink into the sand. Swift, on the other hand, is slower and less sure-footed. The Unenlagiines split up, and one of them weaves past him and runs off, back to the forest. The other Unenlagiine moves farther down the beach.

Tired, Swift does not think of continuing. Australovenators do not perform well in long chases, and the exertion of trying to keep track of these highly nimble targets has taken its toll. The Unenlagiine, victorious, calls out, as it backs away. Keeping its eyes on Swift all the time, to make sure he does not try to resume the chase, it wanders out on the beach.

It is entirely unaware that, about a hundred meters away, a Ferrodraco has launched itself into the air. Although primarily fish eaters, they will not turn down an opportunity for an east meal. Powerful downstrokes carry it across the sand, the noise of its flapping wings blending in with the cries of fishing Ferrodraco and the bellows of the distant Savannasaurus. The Unenlagiine doesn't realize it is coming until seconds before its jaws close around its waist. The Ferrodraco, much larger than the Unenlagiine, lifts it into the air, gripping it in its jaws. However, the Ferrodraco's neck muscles will not be able to support the dinosaur, which fights back vigorously, for too long, and it is forced to land some distance away from Swift.

Dropping the Unenlagiine on the ground, it bites the dinosaur again, and again. The dying animal's screams attract the attention of the many other Ferrodraco gathered on the beach. They take off, flapping towards the Ferrodraco with the downed Unenlagiine. In less than a minute, half a dozen Ferrodraco are gathered around the dying Unenlagiine. Working together, they kill it quickly. The inevitable fight then breaks out, as the Ferrodraco peck and squawk, trying to muscle each other out of the way.

From a distance, Swift watches. He has not taken on this many pterosaurs before. As his stomach gurgles, however, he is reminded that he has nothing left to lose. Desperation can easily turn into confidence, and it is with confidence and surety that Swift marches towards them. He has no other choice. Might as well hold his head high about it.

Swift bellows. A deep, throaty warble. The Ferrodraco fall back and then unite their ranks. Some split off from the rest, to try and circle around him, leaving three Ferrodraco in front of the Unenlagiine. Swift charges, and the three Ferrodraco guarding the carcass realize he will not stop. They flap away, and he finds himself with the Unenlagiine beneath him. However, the Ferrodraco land, and, all six of them together, encircle him. Swift picks the carcass up and turns to leave. A Ferrodraco jumps up and bits him near the base of his tail. He turns and hisses in pain and frustration. Blood drips from the stinging would. Another one, behind him, jumps and bites him in the side. Swift drops the carcass, and the Ferrodraco backs off.

In the distance, a group of Savannasaurus watch. The juvenile, in particular, is drawn by the action and observes attentively.

The Ferrodraco squawk and squabble. Swift stands over the carcass, claws ready. As long as his hands are free, they will not attack. The moment he turns his attention away from them, be it to pick up the carcass or begin tearing food from it with his teeth, they will resume their onslaught. Swift watches them, looking at their beady eyes. He sees one, whose long teeth drip with blood. His blood. Anger fills him. Anger, and frustration, and pain. However, there is nothing he can do. As long as he is ready for a fight, they will not engage him in one. So he reaches down and puts his hands on the carcass. Sensing, an opportunity, one of the Ferrodraco lunges at his side.

And Swift is ready for it. Swinging his body, he slams into it, driving the back of his right hand firmly into its jaw. Dazed, the Ferrodraco falls to the ground and scrambles to get away. Swift abandons the carcass and moves towards it. It manages to get in position to take off, with its forelimbs planted firmly on the ground. If it manages to catapult itself into the air, it will be free. But Swift doesn't let that happen. He hooks his claws into its back and throws it to the ground. He then bites down hard on its neck. The pterosaur screeches in pain, and then its neck is snapped.

Swift turns back to the other Ferrodraco. During the commotion, one of them tried to get the carcass and take off. However, two others saw this and attacked, preventing it from stealing the carcass. Swift charges the three of them, and they scatter. They land a distance away, and Swift hisses loudly. Seeing the dead Ferrodraco, they finally retreat. At last, Swift is left alone with the kills, and at last, he has established himself as the top predator in the area.

But his struggles are far from over.

Chapter 5

Days have passed. Swift's hunger has returned with a passion and gnaws away at his insides. As he rests in a clearing, he begins to question his survival here. There is still no sign of Ornithopods in these forests. It seems the unique coastal environment here favors large herbivores and very small dinosaurs, with little in-between. For a large predator like Swift, finding food will be hard. The small animals are nimble and not very filling. Though fish are plentiful, the water holds monsters. Swift's escape was lucky. He will not risk it again.

The only other potential source of food then is the Savannasaurus. Adults are out of the question; whereas fishing is risky, attacking an adult Savannasaurus is suicidal. However, perhaps a juvenile… If one can be killed, then that would sustain Swift for weeks, if not months.

Swift is hesitant about that plan. Young Savannasaurus are still dangerous prey, and, most importantly, not ones he is accustomed to hunting. But is there another option? Leaving these lands runs the risk of encountering other Australovenators. Given the vastness of Australovenator territories, this stretch of coastal land may be the only area for hundreds of kilometers around that isn't home to Australovenators.

There is no other option. Savannasaurus it is. Swift reluctantly gets to his feet. He stretches and shakes his body, fluffing his feathers and flinging some twigs and dirt from his body. He yawns, opening his mouth wide and exposing his teeth. He then walks off, heading for the place he knows Savannasaurus will be. The beach.

Swift steps out on the beach. The early afternoon sand brings a familiar warmth to his feet. He walks out into the middle of the sandy expanse.

In the distance, the Ferrodraco glide over the sea, searching for fish. To his right, and further down the beach, a group of Savannasaurus browses from the treetops. Swift looks closely. A juvenile wanders about near the adults, moving from one low-hanging ginkgo tree to the next, browsing. A potential target. Swift will need to be cautious, however, and he will need the element of surprise on his side. That, however, is what he is best at. He can do surprise.

He turns and walks off the sand and back into the trees bordering the beach. Hidden in the shadows of the woods, he walks alongside the beach towards the Savannasaurus. The juvenile Savannasaurus comes into sight. Swift slows down. If he is spotted, it may all be over. Silently, he edges closer and closer to it. Eventually, he stops. He will not advance any more, for the juvenile Savannasaurus is still close to the adults. He only stands a chance if the juvenile leaves their protection and heads towards him.

Swift waits. The adults begin to move away, further down the beach. The juvenile, however, is not paying attention. It continues browsing in the same spot as the adults walk away. Perhaps this will work too. All that matters is that the juvenile is not close to the adults. If they intervene, Swift would surely be risking his life. The juvenile then turns to look at the adults. Its attention diverted, Swift seizes the opportunity.

He runs. Deftly leaping over the undergrowth, he dashes closer and closer to the juvenile Savannasaurus. It turns and looks his way. The sound has interested it, but it is not spooked yet. That is good. Swift breaks from the cover of the trees and runs out on the beach, finding himself only a few meters away from the young titanosaur. Now close, he can finally judge the nature of his target. 8 meters long – longer than he is. A moment of doubt and worry flashes through his mind; maybe he has bitten off more than he can chew.

The Savannasaurus lets out a low call. It has realized that it is in danger. It begins turning its body towards the adults. Swift assumes this is because it wants to run back to them. In reality, this is only half the reason. The titanosaur is positioning itself with its tail facing Swift, as its tail is its best weapon. However, the titanosaur's motion reminds Swift that he has come too far for doubts, and decides to go for it. He dashes forward, going around the Savannasaurus. He is heading for the neck of the creature.

The head comes into view, and Swift locks on. He jumps up, trying to bite its head, assuming that is where the damage will be greatest. While he is right in assuming so, the Savannasaurus lifts its head up, and Swift's jaws close around thin air. He readies himself for another lunge, fixing his stance. The Savannasaurus turns again. Facing a predator head-on is not the best option for a titanosaur like it, and so it tries to get into position to use its tail. As it turns, it exposes its right side. Swift notices the base of its neck and decides to try there.

He lunges forward and bites down on the neck, near the shoulder. Here, close to the neck joint, swinging its neck does not help the Savannasaurus. It shakes its body, trying to dislodge the predator. Swift begins to feel his bite weaken. The Savannasaurus then gives one massive shake of its body, throwing its weight to the left, away from him. Swift loses his grip and falls to the ground, landing ungainly on the rough sand. His head lands near the Savannasaurus' feet. The Savannasaurus reacts quickly. It lifts its left leg up and moves its foot into position over Swift's head. Swift's eyes widen as he realizes what is about to happen. He rolls over quickly, and the Savannasaurus' foot just misses his head as it is brought down. Swift scrambles to his feet. Sand covers his feathers, but the adrenaline racing through him means he does not notice.

The Savannasaurus is in a spot of trouble. Having tried to stomp down on Swift's head and having missed, its foot has sunk deep into the sand. As it struggles to free its leg, it thrashes its neck. Swift watches. He readies himself for another strike, but its neck is moving too much. He will not be able to land a secure bite.

And then the Savannasaurus frees itself. In an instant, the tables turn. The Savannasaurus positions itself firmly on the ground and swings its tail and hips to the right. As it does so, it swings its shoulders and neck to the left. This turns its entire front half into a swinging beam, swaying with incredible momentum. Swift has no time to react as the Savannasaurus slams its neck into his chest. He is flung backward, and lands winded. He groans, a pale throaty groan, as he shakes his head, dizzy. The Savannasaurus turns and ambles away. Swift gets to his feet, despite the pain coursing through him. Standing up, he finds himself face to face with a steadily approaching trio of adults. They march towards him, and he backs away, unsteady on his feet. The hunt is over. The Savannasaurus, although lightly wounded, will recover, and Swift's efforts have only brought him pain. Attempting to continue now would be certain death; a kick from an adult would be crippling. He turns and plods back to the forest as the Savannasaurus reunite.

Swift lounges in the creek. The cool water soothes his wounds and washes away the sand from his feathers. From the trees, the telltale sounds of the Unenlagiines emanate. They will not approach as long as he is literally in their water source. Swift does not care, however. His mind is racing. He needs to figure out a new plan and fast. Although wounded, the experience has helped him learn. The Savannasaurus are dangerous opponents. Their necks must be attacked with caution, and their size itself is indeed an active threat, providing great force to all their blows. Swift's relatively weak jaws will not stand against the thrashing of a scared Savannasaurus.

The sun is beginning to descend towards the sea. The sky is not dark yet, but it will be soon. Swift is wounded, and he has a bit more time until he needs to feed again. He will wait until tomorrow.

The sky is on fire. Looking up through the treetops, Swift sees a soft orange hue. Intrigued, he gets up. The water drips from his body, and he shakes himself, spraying it everywhere. He walks out of the creek and back onto dry land, and marches towards the beach.

The sand on the beach is a creamy-beige, and the trees by the beach are painted gold. The shadows of the Savannasaurus on the beach stretch out into the forest. Swift emerges from the trees and out into this glowing world. The big blue of the sea is darker than ever and is cut in half by a thick line of shining orange. A beautiful line, shimmering and sparkling as the waves move across the water. And at the far end of this line, just above the water, a golden globe hovers. Shapes flit across it; the last of the Ferrodraco that have flown out today, still looking for a catch.

Swift's brown feathers shine like those of a Phoenix in the face of the dying sun. He sits down and watches. In the closing moments of the day, peace truly descends over the beach.

The sun dips below the waves. The sky turns into a myriad of colors, from blues to purples to reds. And then the sun disappears, and the day is done. Twilight blankets this cretaceous world. Stars begin to appear, dotting the sky. The prehistoric moon shines down on a quiet land. The Savannasaurus sleep in the distance, and Swift lays his head down to rest.

Early in the morning. The sky is dark, and the stars still bright. The beach is held in a light, calm silence. Then, animals begin to stir. A few Ferrodraco call out, surprised. Soon, Savannasaurus join in the chorus. Swift's eyes slowly open, his eyelids prised apart by the noise. And then, they jolt open as they realize that the sky has come alive. The once dark sky is now filled with the most incredible colors. Bright green, brighter than anything Swift has seen before. Reds and blues dance above the green ribbons, in a mosaic of smoke-like color. The Aurora Australis.

Almost 150 million kilometers away, the sun is continuously emitting a stream of charged particles – the Solar Wind. As these reach the Earth, they generate a magnetic storm in the upper atmosphere. Charged particles race and weave through the air a hundred kilometers above the beach. The end result, for the dinosaurs standing below, is a beautiful display of light and color floating in the sky. As the sea reflects the weaving lights, Swift finds himself on a beach between skies. Indescribable beauty above and below him.

Several minutes pass with the lights swirling above the dinosaurs' heads. The concerned calls of the dinosaurs fade and all that remains in the thick night air is a wondrous silence as the noiseless display continues. Slowly, the lights begin to thin and fade. A few streaks of bright green remain, and then they too disappear into the dark sky. The excitement and awe over, the creatures' fatigue sets in again. The beach is quiet again, and Swift lies down too. As he is overtaken by the need to sleep, his eyes close once again, but the beauty he has seen tonight will not be forgotten.

Morning. Swift rises. Around him, activity has resumed as usual. The Savannasaurus plod around the beach. Nearby, a Ferrodraco catapults itself into the air, off to join its kin who have already taken off for the day's fishing. Swift will have work to do too, and so he turns away from the beach and heads back towards his usual morning spot, the creek. He quickly quenches his thirst and then walks off in the direction of the beach.

From the forest's edge, he prowls alongside the beach. He smells the air and finds the scent that he is looking for. Blood. Dried blood. Following it, he heads towards the juvenile Savannasaurus. Its wound is healing, but the blood still marks the spot. Swift watches, keeping his distance. He will wait for it to leave the safety of the others once more, and then he will try to finish what he started.

Midday. Several Ferrodraco, who have already made a catch, have returned to the beach and bask in the sunlight. Although the shade of the trees is inviting, they are wary of approaching the forest. If they were to tear the skin of their wings on the branches, they might not be able to fly again until it heals. Also, with a 4-meter wingspan, takeoff within the forest is extremely difficult. They are not willing to take the risk of being grounded in the forest, where a hungry dinosaur would have the upper hand.

At the beach's edge, Swift lies below the treetops. He lies in waiting. A short distance away is the young Savannasaurus. It has distanced itself from the adults, but Swift is patient. He will not attack yet. He wants to have as much time to do as much damage as possible before the adults can reach the juvenile.

The juvenile is nervous. It is still shaken from its previous encounter with Swift and is aware that its wound may attract unwanted attention. However, with an ever-present need to eat, hunger drives the juvenile to keep browsing, even as the nearby adults have wandered off to browse from taller trees.

Swift decides it is time. He gets to his feet and approaches the beach slowly. His eyes are locked on the wound at the base of its neck. A new plan that he has been working on ever since the previous encounter is lodged in his brain.

The Savannasaurus continues browsing. Suddenly, it hears the sound of running on the sand. It turns to look, as Swift closes in on it. Before the Savannasaurus can react, Swift bites it on the wound. It calls out in pain and begins shaking itself. This time, Swift knows he will not be able to hold on forever, so he lets go. His footing still secure; he backs away slightly.

The Savannasaurus turns itself, trying to get its tail in position as a defensive mechanism. If it does, it will all be over for Swift. So he dashes forward and nips at the base of the neck, tearing off some flesh. He then moves slightly forward, so that his shoulder is now near the wound. Raising his arm up, he pulls his claws back and brings them down on its neck. They cut through the wounded flesh, leaving great gashes.

Swift then lunges again, landing quick bites further up the Savannasaurus' neck. However, he overplays his hand and has gotten too close for too long. The Savannasaurus swings its weight towards the Australovenator, and Swift is rammed by its shoulder, the osteoderms slamming into his side. He comes crashing down, and here, near the forest's edge, the sand is not soft, and is mixed with soil and branches. Pain flashing through his shoulder, it takes him a few seconds to get up. When he does so, he sees the juvenile is trudging off through the sand as quickly as it can. Moving towards it are the adults. However, the sand slows down their progress, and Swift still has time.

Giving chase, he runs up to the Savannasaurus' left side. He lifts his right arm up and reaches up and over the Savannasaurus' back. Grabbing it, he holds on, in a sort of sideways-hug. Due to the Savannasaurus' height, he can only hop along on one leg as he is carried along by the titanosaur. He bites its neck again, and the Savannasaurus struggles to shake him off. Carried by its momentum, its mental efforts are directed towards moving in a straight line and maintaining its balance. However, as the pain from its neck becomes too much to bear, it swings its body sideways as it runs. Swift is thrown off and falls back down. However, the Savannasaurus' concentration is momentarily broken, and it stumbles. Unable to react quickly, and unable to correct its footing in the soft sand, its momentum carries it forwards, and it falls, chest-down.

Swift gets to his feet as the adults close in. The juvenile moans, tired from its wounds and the exertion of the fight. Swift contemplates trying to continue attacking, but the angry calls of the adults are a reminder that he must back off soon.

And so he does. Slowly, he backs away, and then turns and starts walking off. He looks back at the juvenile, who continues lying there. Finally, for the first time since arriving here, confidence starts flowing through him. His prey is badly wounded. The hunt may have been successful.

Nightfall comes, and Swift's hopes are confirmed. The juvenile Savannasaurus gives in to its wounds and dies. The adults leave it. This is merely the way of the natural world, and they have no reason to mourn. Under cover of darkness, Swift moves onto the beach and towards his kill. His tiredness is overcome by the promise of a full meal, something he has not had since leaving his former territory. That night, he gorges himself.

During the days and nights to come, until he needs to eat again, he stays by the carcass, guarding it. Its meat can sustain him for over a month. Around him, life goes on. The Savannasaurus go about their business, knowing that he is no threat to them now that he has food. The Ferrodraco keep their distance. They know what he is capable of. Whenever he goes to the creek, they swarm the carcass, trying to rip meat off it as best they can, but when he returns, they scatter. Swift has established himself as the top predator here. Against all the odds, he has managed to find his place in this strange land.

ns Swift

Part Two: The Science

The continent of Australia 95 million years ago would have been very different from the one we know today. The continent was much farther south, and the weather was cooler and wetter. In the middle of Australia, there was a vast inland sea known as the Eromanga Sea. The Eromanga Sea, which had already been present for many millions of years, was fading 95 million years ago, and on the brink of disappearance. As its waters receded, the vast areas around it became wet and filled with large rivers and lakes. The forests of the Winton Formation would have been moist and tropical.

However, it was not always like this. Evidence from the sediment shows that there was a lot of variation in the temperature and weather of the region. The temperature would have ranged throughout the year between a slightly hot 20 degrees Celsius and a chilly 7 degrees Celsius in the winter months, and there was a cycle of drier and wetter years, with some periods of relative dryness extending over several years. It is during one such drier period, where the land may have been a little less plentiful than usual, that the story of Banjo and Swift's adult lives is set.

The Eromanga Sea and its coastline are the main setting of Part 2 of the story, and one of its inhabitants was a truly awesome creature. In 1899, the first remains of a giant aquatic animal were discovered, and in 1924 it was named *Kronosaurus queenslandicus*. Ever since then, more remains of this creature have continued to be unearthed.

Kronosaurus was a large, four-flippered marine reptile, belonging to a group of reptiles called Pliosaurs. Interestingly, the question of Kronosaurus' body size forms a good example of how paleontology yields results that constantly develop and improve as knowledge grows. In 1959, its size was estimated at 12.4 meters long and weighing a massive 17,900 kg. However, since then more knowledge about its relatives and a reinterpretation of the skeletons' condition when found suggests that it had been reconstructed with too many bones in its backbone. Nonetheless, although it was found to be slightly smaller than thought, it was still one of the largest predators of its time, at 10.5-10.9 meters long and weighing a little over 10,000 kg.

In addition, its skull was over 2 meters in length, and its massive teeth could measure up to 30 cm long. Its main prey would have been small and medium sized marine reptiles, such as Plesiosaurs and turtles, and large squid. However, as the Eromanga Sea continued to shrink, its world would have gotten smaller, and its food sources more limited as competition with other Kronosaurus increased. This may have driven it to hunt closer to the shorelines, potentially bringing it into contact with dinosaurs and pterosaurs.

This brings us to the creatures of the Eromanga coastline. Although what coexisted with Australovenator for most of its inland range is known, what animals of the Winton Formation would have inhabited the coastlines is unclear. However, some guesses can be made.

Firstly, Savannasaurus. A very close relative of Diamantinasaurus, but much wider in build, it is shown as living on the coastline for the following reason. A great number of sauropods is known from the Winton Formation; Diamantinasaurus, Wintonotitan, and Savannasaurus are some. Therefore, it is likely that to avoid competition with each other, some of these would have inhabited different areas. The reason why the coastal sauropod was chosen to be Savannasaurus lies in its extreme morphology. It is extremely wide-hipped and wide-chested, giving it a barrel-like shape that has been likened to that of a hippopotamus. This would have given it increased stability when walking across uneven terrain. While this probably evolved to help it navigate the wetlands and rivers of the Winton Formation during its wetter phases, it is also quite possible that this would have helped it adapt to and survive in coastal, sandy environments. This is something that is actually seen in hippos today, where some populations of hippos have taken to living on the atlantic beaches of Gabon.

Another inhabitant of the coastal forests are the small Unenlagiines. Unenlagiines are a group of dinosaurs known from South America, Madagascar, and Australia. The Australian remains are, unfortunately, the poorest remains of Unenlagiines. They are only known from a few bones, and only one of them can be identified as belonging to an Unenlagiine with any confidence. However, there is also another line of evidence suggesting the presence of Unenlagiines in Australia – the high similarity between Australian and South American dinosaurs. Megaraptorans like Australovenator, Titanosaurs like the sauropods from the Winton Formation, and other Australian dinosaurs like Noasaurids are also known in South America. This indicates that Australia and South America were connected at some point before the Winton Formation. This, combined with the potential Unenlagiine bones from southern Australia, suggests Unenlagiines may likely have made it to Australia. Although some Unenlagiines are known to have been quite large, such as the 6-meter long Austroraptor, the majority were small animals around a meter in length. This is why the Australian Unenlagiines shown here are not very large – and being small animals, they fit well in the dense forests of the coast of the Eromanga Sea. Their probable diets (based on their relatives that have skull bones preserved) would also support this, since they likely preyed on insects, lizards, and probably even fish, which would have been present along the coastline.

Ferrodraco is the most recently discovered creature shown in the coastal lands, having been found in April 2017, and described and named in October 2019. It belonged to a group of pterosaurs called Ornithocheirids, a truly global group of pterosaurs known from South America, Africa, England, and Australia. Like other Ornithocheirids, it would have primarily hunted fish, although it would have had no problem eating other animals such as small dinosaurs given the chance. Given its fish-eating diet, it is quite likely that some populations of Ferrodraco would have lived around the shrinking Eromanga sea, even though the only Ferrodraco specimen known so far was found in a more inland environment, likely hunting around large lakes and rivers.

Ornithopods are left absent from the coastline on account of their body plan. The ones in the Winton Formation were likely cursorial animals, adapted towards speed. Moreover, their small size meant that speed would be their main defence against predators like Australovenator. These attributes would be of great help to them on open plains and lightly forested woods, but in the dense forests of the coast where manoeuvrability is limited and the ground unstable, limiting their speed, their physique would be a hindrance. Therefore, they are not depicted along the Eromanga Sea's coastline.

As mentioned in Part One: The Science, the flora (plant-life) of the Winton Formation is very well-understood. Admittedly it is known primarily from fossil leaves and seeds, which mean we cannot reliably estimate the sizes of its flora beyond looking at their modern relatives, but what we have clearly indicates it was an extremely varied assemblage of plants. This is not entirely unexpected, as the world was experiencing a great turnover in its global flora at the time. Ginkgo trees, a group of plants whose only living member is the species Ginkgo biloba, were very common. So too were the angiosperm plants, more commonly known as flowering plants, which were at the time in intense competition with Ginkgos. In the rest of the world at the time, the angiosperm plants' much more successful means of fruit-based seed dispersal was driving the Ginkgo trees nearly to extinction. Australia was one of the last places where the Ginkgo trees were still diverse, though there too they would disappear almost entirely in time.

Conifer trees, another common and successful type of plant that are still very abundant today, thrived in the Winton Formation. A great variety of fossils from them have been found, from needles to pine cones, but even they would struggle in prehistoric Australia as the angiosperms multiplied in numbers.

Lastly, the presence of Cycads is uncertain, and it is disputed whether some possible Cycad fossils truly belong to Cycads. However, regardless of whether or not the controversial fossils are indeed remains of Cycads, it is always possible that Cycads were present, especially around the rivers and deltas feeding into the Eromanga sea.

Banjo and Swift

Banjo and Swift

Part Three

Banjo and Swift

Chapter 1

One year later. The smooth melody of the creek is punctured by soft splashing. The Unenlagiines have gathered to socialize. Two males spar with each other, nipping and clawing playfully. A female and her mate sit together, watching the others. A juvenile, less than a meter long, hops around, under the watchful eye of its parent. A small dragonfly darts about over the creek, its wings as transparent as the water's surface.

The glistening green insect flits over to the edge of the creek, catching the attention of the juvenile Unenlagiine, which turns nimbly, hopping after it. It stands little chance of catching it, but the practice is useful. Though only a year old, it is almost as agile as an adult. It is inexperienced, however, and as the insect swerves, the young dinosaur loses its balance and falls. It gets up quickly and shakes its head. Frustrated, but enjoying this practice, it runs after the insect.

On the other side of the creek, Swift lies. The Unenlagiines no longer fear him. He has eaten well; a Savannasaurus he killed over a month ago still fills his stomach. With another food source available, he no longer considers the small Unenlagiines as prey. As a result, they do not consider him a threat.

Swift has done well for himself. He is plump and well-fed and still manages to remain fit. Although the vast expanses of dry land he once used to run in are miles away, the beach suffices as a training ground. All thoughts of struggling to survive are gone from his mind. However, for months now, the second challenge of life grows strong within him. It is not hunger which now gnaws his insides, but desire. The desire, the need, to mate. To pass on his genes and bear offspring.

Bordered by the sea, and surrounded by many large territories, the chances of encountering a female are slim. To get to his area, she must pass through those of many other Australovenators. Some will not be inviting, ruled over by mated pairs. Others will be too inviting, with other lone males whom the female would be more than happy to settle down with.

If Swift could sigh, he would. Sluggishly, he gets to his feet. Out of habit, the Unenlagiines stop for a second and then get back to their play. Swift towers above them, 4 times their height, and looks at them. His brain has no way of comprehending their happiness, their contentment at being with others of their kind. Still, perhaps something in seeing so many predatory dinosaurs, like miniature versions of himself in a way, grouped together, makes him pause for a second.

The second passes, and Swift turns away from them. Off he lumbers back into the forest. Familiar bird cries drone on as he marches over the floor, littered with branches and twigs. Up ahead, the bright blue sky frames the tree trunks. Back out onto the beach he steps. Familiar sand between his toes. Savannasaurus browse in the distance, and Ferrodraco laze about nearby. Swift doesn't look at them; he knows they are there as always.

He looks out to sea, the last source of mystery left. He knows there are creatures beneath the waves he has no comprehension of. Worlds of fish and giants. A breeze ruffles his feathers. He inhales, breathing in the familiar smell of the salty water. He sits down, staring forward. The Ferrodraco dance above the waves. Their powerful flight, and intricate aerial ability, is a sight Swift has come to appreciate. The beauty of their movement is not lost on him.

And then a smell reaches him. Swift is puzzled. This is not a scent from his territory. This is something new. Swift inhales again. No. Not new. This is old. Very old. Not a new smell, but one that was forgotten. As Swift realizes what that smell signifies, he leaps to his feet, joyous.

An Australovenator. This means two possibilities. An intruder, or a female. Out of longing, Swift instantly forgets the former possibility and latches on to the second one. A mate. At last.

Swift turns quickly and faces the forest. He sniffs eagerly and picks up the scent. The calls of the other animals are practically muted, nothing more than background noise. With confidence, Swift struts back into the forest. He moves beneath the shade of the trees, following the scent trail.

The sun begins to descend. As it slowly moves closer and closer to the sea, Swift has made no progress. He has scoured the forest, but the female has not been found. The beach is clear too. Perhaps Swift just keeps missing her. He contemplates calling out but does not want to spook her either. Then, Swift is hit by a realization. As thirst begins to swell up in his throat, he finds himself walking, out of habit, in the direction of the creek. Perhaps that is the best course of action. All animals need to drink. If the female is still here, she may go there too.

Out over the sea, the sun is almost kissing the water's surface. Golden rays from the dying day pierce between the branches of the trees. Above the canopy, the sky is burning. On the creek, beams of light strike the rippling water, and the usually clear surface becomes speckled with gold.

Swift lies a distance away from the creek, observing. A couple of Unenlagiines rest in the dying sunlight, their feathers dappled with tints of orange. A sadness begins to fill Swift's heart. Doubt starts to grow. Perhaps the female has indeed moved on.

And then the Unenlagiines perk up. Quickly, they get to their feet and scatter, running off. Within seconds, they are gone, and the area around the creek is still. Silence, save for the tinkling of the water. Then, a crack in the forest. Swift watches like a hawk. Movement in the trees. A rustling of leaves, not from wind, but from something brushing against the branches. Beams of light ripple and crackle as something large moves through them, casting new shadows. Then, out of the cover of the trees and into the light steps an Australovenator. It looks around, then lowers its head and drinks from the cool water.

Swift looks, searching for an indication as to the sex of the Australovenator. In the low light conditions, Swift cannot make out the feathering on its tail. Worried his chance may slip away, he bites the bullet and gets to his feet. The Australovenator tenses, having noticed the movement in the forest.

Swift emerges, his body held low to the ground. He leans forward, raising his tail. A submissive gesture. The other Australovenator watches, still tense. Swift turns himself sideways, showing the white feathering on his tail. The other Australovenator understands this is a sign that Swift is interested, but is hesitant to return the gesture.

Swift waits. He knows it is best not to rush things. The other Australovenator contemplates this. Then, it turns sideways too. Joy fills Swift as he sees that there is no white feathering on the other's tail. A female. Swift's heart beats in his chest. Adrenaline rushes through him. For the first time in a year, the urge to mate now drives him forward. He steps into the creek, advancing towards the female. She backs off slightly, but she isn't spooked. She is merely making sure she does not appear too interested. She has yet to see what Swift has to offer.

The gold fades from the ripples on the creek as the sun begins to dip behind the horizon. Streaks of light still paint the trees and the enraptured dinosaurs' feathers. Over the stream, bugs start to gather and swarm, flitting through the evening air like specks in the wind. As their silver wings reflect the light, they glisten like miniature stars orbiting an invisible planet. They, too, are mating. These insects have their own lives and struggles, just on an infinitely smaller scale than the two Australovenators, who are so colossal the tiny insects do not even know they are there.

Likewise, neither of the Australovenators is aware of the presence of the insects, for they are too tiny, and the dinosaurs too captivated. Swift takes another step, and the surface of the creek ripples outwards, bouncing off the banks and merging with the ripples of the female as she too steps into the creek.

They begin to circle each other, their toes dipped into the cool water. The female avoids eye contact, looking at his body instead. The setting sun glints in Swift's eyes as half a circle is completed. The female watches his legs. She watches to see his muscles pull and stretch, attempting to calculate his strength and speed. A circle is complete, and the sunset is back behind Swift. His silhouette is projected onto the female's glowing body. They do not stop, continuing their appraisal of each other in this dance at the close of day.

The sun dips below the sea. The bugs quieten down and disperse. Above the creek, the purpling sky begins to glitter. The shadows stretching out across the forest floor blur and soon fade into a general darkness over the ground.

The circling stops. The female stands still, observing Swift. Swift turns his body to face her. The water of the creek now runs colder, chilling his feet. Swift lets out a low, long, drawn-out warble. It carries through the still air, on to the beach, and throughout the forest. Swift lowers himself in a submissive pose. He wants the female to know she has the power of choice here. He opens his mouth, hissing softly. He turns his open maw up to the female, showing her the rows of teeth concealed within. He begins sidestepping across the water, always facing her. He stops, and paws the creek with his feet, rippling the water's surface.

The female continues observing, completely still, not betraying any of her thoughts and emotions in her stance. Swift rears up. He straightens his legs as much as he can, and leans back, lowering his tail until it swings low above the surface of the running water. He raises his neck up and stretches out his arms. Without his brother to overshadow him, hesitation and self-doubt do not hold him back.

He stands like that for a few seconds and then looks down at the female. She returns his gaze. Their eyes are locked. He begins to approach her, lowering his body slowly until his head is only slightly above hers.

She turns away. As the dance went on, so did twilight, and darkness has begun to creep through the forest. Without good lighting, the female is hesitant to push the matter. She wanders off through the woods, away from the creek. Swift watches her go for a moment. He then snaps out of his longing reverie, and follows her, moving through the forest after her.

He catches up to her at the beach. She stands out on the sands, staring out to sea, as he did when first observing the coastal night. The darkened waves are tipped with white, from the bright moon's light. The incredible quiet hits Swift like a powerful gust of wind, and he joins the female in her immobile state. Staring out across the beach, as a gentle, cool breeze blows across the sand.

He approaches the female. He is casual; this is not an attempt to woo her. Knowing this, she turns and faces him. A friendly gesture. Even if she proves not interested in finding a mate, she is, for the time being, happy to have encountered another of her kind. At least one who is not hostile towards her. The feeling is shared by Swift. Memories of the pain inflicted by his brother are gone. In this moment, there is only each other. Two wild creatures, nomads in this ancient world, together in this strange land. The lapping of the waves, the rustling of leaves. Nothing else. Darkness on the ground, with lights above. A little bubble around these two souls.

They lie down together. Below the stars, sleep begins overtaking them. Though they keep their distance from each other, as their consciousness drifts away, each other's presence is felt. And it is lovely.

Chapter 2

Morning. Swift slowly opens his eyelids, awoken by the sounds of the Ferrodraco flying out to fish. Sluggishly, still getting to his sense, he turns to look to his right. The female is nowhere to be seen. He sighs, then brings himself to his feet. Perhaps she rose early, still unaccustomed to the area, and wary of any potential threats.

Swift stands on the beach, looking out to sea. High tide, and the water laps just a few meters away from him. A few moments later, having regained his strength, he turns and walks back into the forest, guessing where the female may have gone.

His guess proves correct. She is lying among the low-growing plants a short distance away from the creek. Like him, she knows watering spots are the best place to stake out if you want to observe the local wildlife. He approaches her, slowly, head bowed. She faces him, acknowledging his presence. He calls to her, a low, friendly call. She does not return it. During the day, she will be cautious about appearing too friendly. She knows he may attempt to win her over; he may already be attempting to.

Swift stops moving and stands near her. She turns and looks out at the creek, and he goes to watch too. The Unenlagiines have not emerged; they are nervous, now that a new Australovenator has arrived. As a result, the female is hesitant to move. She wants to observe and keep a low profile.

Swift decides to break the standstill and moves towards the creek. He drinks, aware that the female's eye will be on him. He turns to look at her casually and sees her still sitting there, cautious. He sits down by the creek, his back to her. Like her, he can play the waiting game. He knows she will need to drink, but also that curiosity and the longing to be with her kind, as demonstrated last night, will draw her out.

Once again, he is proven right. He hears the cracking of twigs and footsteps on the dry ground. Without turning, he knows she is coming out to drink. She comes into view on his right, stooping down and taking in some water. She then sits near him. Next to him, but not too close. Still keeping her distance. Swift waits a few minutes, enjoying her company. Then, he gets to his feet. He cannot afford to miss an opening.

He walks through the creek and onto the opposite bank. The female, still seated, watches him. He turns to check on her, and they lock eyes. That is good. The progress made yesterday at sundown has not been lost. He lets out his low, melodious warble. She cocks her head to the side, listening. Silence follows. She doesn't make a sound.

Steeling himself, Swift begins the routine. On solid ground this time, he paws the ground. He opens his mouth as wide as possible and lets out a loud call. It is long, and resonating, vibrating deep within the female as she sits on the other side of the creek. He jumps up and lands down with both his feet. On the soft creek-side soil, however, it does not make much noise. Swift takes this information and adjusts his plans accordingly. He jumps again, but this time jumps forward, landing loudly in the creek.

He stretches his arms out and swings his body left to right. A display of strength. He looks at the female curiously. She isn't buying it. She is aware, he realizes, that his size and stature are subpar for an Australovenator. He will need to display something new to her.

He walks back, out of the creek and onto the bank. There, on solid footing, he rears up, stretching to his full height. And he raises his right leg. Shifting his tail and body weight slightly, to balance, he maintains that pose, one leg raised off the ground. The female watches, somewhat intrigued. Her interest grows the longer he stays like this, one foot on the ground.

He then lowers his foot and switches leg, standing on his right leg now. He looks down at the female, calling to her. She stands up and moves towards him. Into the creek she walks, until she stands in the middle of the rippling water.

She looks at him. Eye contact is made. Swift stares deep into her eyes, and she stares back. She feels the same as he does. Staring at her body language, and into those eyes, Swift is sure at last that she is looking for a mate. However, almost with a hint of sadness, she turns away from him. Although his performance has impressed her, his physical attributes are not the greatest, and the survival of her offspring depends on a capable father. She turns and walks off, moving down the creek. Down to the beach. She is not leaving his territory yet, so there is still a chance. Swift has not been rebuffed; the female is merely hesitant to accept him.

He watches her leave, and then, when she is a safe distance away, Swift follows, making sure not to get too close. He does not want to overwhelm her now. Her peace of mind is the most important thing to him.

As they leave the creek, the Unenlagiines return. The young juvenile splashes around near the edges of the stream. The mated pair sit in the shade of a large tree, watching their playful kin. One Unenlagiine looks down the creek, watching the two lumbering giants move away.

The female steps out from the trees and onto the beach. She sits down on the sand, pensive. The Savannasaurus calls grab her attention for a second. She turns and looks at them, and, seeing that they are some distance away, she looks back out to sea and pays them no more attention.

From the cover of the trees, Swift watches. He is not trying to remain hidden, he merely wishes not to be intrusive. Slowly, he walks out of the forest and towards the female. He appears to her left, and she glances at him, startled. He stops and lowers his body, and she looks away, seeing that he means no harm.

He moves forward and goes in front of her, standing between her and the waves. She looks up at him, and he calls out to her. A friendly call this time. She merely lowers her head and faces away from him. Swift's head hangs low. He needs to find some way to impress her, to show off his true potential. A Ferrodraco calls out behind him. He turns and looks out at it, gliding above the water's surface.

It dives down and disappears in a splash. A few seconds later, it bursts back out in a spray of seafoam. Swift follows it with his eyes as it flies off. He then turns his gaze back to the sea in front of him. From the corner of her eye, the female glances at him.

Thoughts run through Swift's mind. Thoughts of danger and risk. Thoughts of reward and potential. He flexes his fingers and inhales, breathing in the salty sea air. The sea's surface is light blue above the sandy shallows, and the waves are calm and gentle.

Swift steps forward. One step after another, he moves towards the sea. The female watches him as he walks away from her. His feet then meet the cool water, but he does not stop walking. Into the waves he wades, and the female perks up. She gets to her feet as he walks off, going further and further out to sea. She moves towards him, approaching the sea, and stops just beyond the water-line. Swift marches on, assuredly. Out into the big blue.

Chapter 3

Earlier that morning. The sun breaks above the horizon, somewhere far behind the forest. A Ferrodraco opens her eyes. Lying sprawled out on the beach, she clambers to her feet. She shakes her head and clacks her beak. She lets out a raspy call, welcoming the day. Sand is speckled over her underside, caught in her fur-like pycnofibres. Eager to get rid of the itching, she wades into the water. Straying only a few dozen meters off-shore, until the water reaches her shoulders, she lowers herself and shakes about in the water.

Properly cleaned, she goes back onto the sand and shakes herself, getting rid of some of the water. Balancing on one arm, she stretches out the other, checking on the long flap of skin that forms her wing. She repeats the process on the other arm. Stretched and ready to go, the old female prepares herself for another day on the wing.

She gets into position and pushes down with her arms. One moment of exertion, and then she is in the air, gliding effortlessly. The light blue water below her darkens as she flies further out to sea. During the start of the day, she will scour the deeper parts of the sea for fish. In the later hours, she will go closer to the shoreline and look for fish there.

Her eyes, like the Australovenators', are very powerful, and she scans the water's surface for the glistening of fish scales. However, today she will not need to spot fish. Her neighbors will do it for her. Nearby, there is a commotion, as a couple of Ferrodraco dive in and out of the water. The old female flies over, adjusting and bending her arms to turn. Looking down, she sees a shoal of fish near the water's surface. They were presumably scared up there by some aquatic predator, hunting below them. Aquatic fish-eating predators often employ this tactic, herding shoals of fish up towards the surface, trapping them.

The female Ferrodraco dives down to try and take part in the feeding frenzy. Her first dive finds her in the midst of the fish, which scatter before her. She swims after them, using her wings as makeshift flippers, and paddling with her legs. Not very efficient and not graceful in the slightest, but it gets the job done. It's a technique many pterosaurs like Ferrodraco employ.

Soon, she runs out of oxygen and swims up towards the surface. She takes off from the water in three powerful strokes, gains height, and dives again. Unfortunately, she is unlucky. The aquatic predator that was hunting the fish has eaten its fill and moved on. As a result, the shoal of fish sinks to lower depths, out of the Ferrodraco's reach. She will need to search elsewhere for today's meal.

Off she goes. A few flaps of her wings give her speed, and then she glides above the sea, scouring the water. Around her swoop other Ferrodraco, each going about the same daily struggle. On the wing, there are no predators, so it is not a very tense life. Nonetheless, finding food is a challenge, and it is one they go through day after day.

A little after midday. The female Ferrodraco managed to make a catch a few hours ago and has gone back to fish closer to the beach. She glides across the waves, about a hundred meters away from the shoreline. On the beach, Swift watches her. Behind him, the female Australovenator lies, watching him from the corner of her eye.

The female Ferrodraco suddenly spots a glittering in the water. A small group of fish. She quickly drops, pulling her wings into a v-shape and diving down. She splashes down into the water in the middle of the fish. She snaps out but misses, and the fish scatter. Empty-mouthed, she takes off again, bursting out of the water. On the beach, Swift follows her flight as she moves across the water.

Swift marches out to sea. On the beach, the female Australovenator watches him. The water level rises, above his knee, eventually reaching his hands. This is as deep as Swift is willing to go. He pulls his hands up. He will not be needing them. Drawing on his memory of last time, he lowers his head close to the water's surface.

He waits as the lukewarm water laps at his legs. Eyes darting around him, he hopes the female's interest will not fade before he has a chance to demonstrate his prowess. As he waits, he tilts his head, flexing his neck. He will need to be quick.

Suddenly, a shimmering of scales catches his eye. A small shape darts around below him. A fish. Not particularly large, but it is worth a shot. Luck is on his side too; the fish is curious and swims into position, near his head. He turns his head slowly, hoping that his shadow does not scare it. The fish seems to be unaware of his presence. With the speed of a heron, he darts forward, burying his head in the water. He feels nothing between his teeth, just the moving of water through his jaws. He pulls back and looks around. The fish is nowhere to be seen. Missed.

Swift is out of practice and rusty. The female's interest was piqued slightly by Swift's attempt, but it will soon fade. Time is of the essence. In more ways than one.

Below the waves, a leviathan moves.

Another attempt is made. Another failure. The female is getting bored. Swift needs to make the next one. A fish comes swims by. Large, and seemingly slow. A good target. Swift lowers his head to the water's surface and opens his jaws. With the calm water, he can get close to the surface without fear of being hit by a wave. His vision becomes impaired as he gets closer; he can only see the fish if it swims within several centimeters of his head.

A splash is heard, coming from about thirty meters away. The female Ferrodraco has also spotted a fish and has dived down to try and grab it. Swift pays no heed to it; all of his attention is focused on his target. He must be ready to strike the moment it comes into view.

And so it does. The shine of it scales alerts Swift to its position, mere centimeters away. It's all or nothing, and Swift swings his head, plunging it into the water. His jaws close down on brittle scales, and his teeth slice through to the soft flesh. The fish flails around in his jaws as he pulls back out of the water, triumphant. He turns back to look at the beach, to see the female standing there, watching him. Quickly, he transfers the fish to his hands, and, his mouth free, he calls out to her.

And then, just as before, the water explodes. About thirty meters away, there is an eruption of spray and foam as the water comes alive. Two meters in length, the colossal head of the Kronosaurus bursts through the surface. Clamped tightly in its jaws is the old female Ferrodraco. She lets out one final, pained call, with the last of her breath. Then the Kronosaurus' head slams back down into the water, and her life is over.

Stillness returns to the water. The Australovenator on the beach is shaken by what she has seen. Swift is still for a few moments, and then he turns away. He knew the risks going in. Soon, his mind moves on, and he remembers the fish held in his hand. He marches back to the beach, his prize in his hands. The female waits for him and welcomes him with an inquisitive call. He rears back and stretches out his arms, offering her the fish. Hesitantly, she reaches forward and nibbles at it. Seeing that it is edible, she takes it in her hands. A few bites later, and the fish is gone.

And then a low, songlike cry leaves her lips. She approaches Swift, staring him in the eyes. She lowers her body; a submissive pose. Swift returns her call. She lowers her head and leans into him, nuzzling him with her forehead. He nips her on the back of her neck lightly, an affectionate bite. She moves closer to him, and they rub bodies, mingling their scents.

That night they lie together on the beach. They are as one, with no distance between them. His neck rests on hers, and their bodies are intertwined beneath the stars. Nomads no more. They do not have many emotions, but tonight, lying together in the cool dark, they are happy. For their kind, this is as close to love as it gets.

Chapter 4

Six months later. It is mating season for the largest residents of the coastal lands; the Savannasaurus. Unlike Australovenators, they do not form lasting bonds. Every year, during the mating season, the males will compete for the attention of the females. The lucky males will be chosen by the females as the fathers of their offspring. A couple of months later, the females will lay their eggs, digging deep holes on the beach with their back legs, and then burying the eggs within the warm sand. They will not guard the eggs. The Unenlagiines are not adapted for eating eggs, and even if they were they would never be able to dig deep enough to reach the buried Savannasaurus eggs.

A male Savannasaurus approaches a solitary female. He lets out a call; the call of a Savannasaurus is a deep bellow, traveling from the chest, through the long neck, and bellowing out of the nose. More like a gigantic hum than a call. The female shows interest and looks him over. There is no complex display system for the Savannasaurus; if the male is physically competent, the female will choose him. More often than not, another male will challenge him for her, and it is then that they can demonstrate their strengths.

The male is young and well-built. Strong legs and muscles, he is taller than she is. He will do. She lets out another call, and stops walking, letting him catch up to her. For Savannasaurus, this counts as acceptance. However, it is never that easy for a male, and, as expected, another Savannasaurus call bellows out.

A slightly older male is marching towards them. He, too, is physically strong, and his age suggests experience. His chances are good. The younger male turns to face him, and they size up to each other. The older male is only slightly taller. The posturing begins, complete with swinging tails and stomping legs. The female watches; she will not choose unless one of the two backs down. Both of the males are strong, however, and they know it. Neither will back down based on posturing alone. A fight is inevitable.

They approach each other, head-on. They line up, somewhat next to each other. Their heads are near each other's shoulders, with their necks held upright and parallel to each other. And then the fight begins. Like great fleshy clubs, they swing their necks at each other, slamming their 6-meter long columns of meat and bone into each other. The sound of each blow is deafening, as the smashing of necks continues.

Eventually, the older male backs down. Inevitably, a stronger opponent turned up, and this is his first loss. The younger male moves towards the female, while the older male moves off. He will try his luck elsewhere; there are plenty more females out here.

Deep within the forest stands one of the only clearings within the deeply-wooded coastal expanse. The large patch of sunlight in the clearing highlights Swift, who lies within it. He is soaking up the warmth and light of the midday sun. He is content and well-fed. His eyes droop lazily, but they are not shut. The reason why he does not sleep is just several meters away. Among the trees on the rim of the clearing, one stands out: a large, old Ginkgo tree, which has spread its branches out and grown its leaves so thickly that only the smallest specks of light glitter in its shade. Beneath the grand tree, gathered among its roots, is a cluster of eggs.

A few fern fronds cover this makeshift nest. A total of 6 eggs are grouped together. All of them Swift's. Within a few weeks, they will hatch. Swift does not expect that all of them will; it is very unlikely for all the embryos within the clutch of an Australovenator to survive. However, those that do survive will be young and covered in downy fluff. Their eyes will betray their intelligence, and their agility and nimbleness will portray their destinies as great hunters.

But for now, the eggs are vulnerable. Granted, there are few predators here, and the Ferrodraco never venture this deep into the forest. Still, Swift does not want to risk a group of Unenlagiines becoming too curious. Therefore, he stands guard, never letting himself fall too deeply asleep.

Out on the beach lies the female. She too is warming up in the midday sun, and she too is guarding something. Behind her lies the carcass of a young Savannasaurus. The two Australovenators have been living off it these past few weeks. Here, the opportunistic Ferrodraco must be held at bay; they will not hesitate to swarm the carcass if the Australovenators leave it for too long. Hence, the two Australovenators have a system. Every couple of days, the one guarding the Savannasaurus will leave it and will go and join the other at the nest. Once reunited at the nest, the other will leave and go to the beach to eat its fill, and then watch over the Savannasaurus carcass. Although they spend so much time apart, the bond between the two mates is strong. As long as they have offspring to raise, they will never even consider leaving the other.

Several hundred kilometers south. Dusty, open desert. The weather here has only worsened over the past year and a half, and the plants are dry and withered. There is no large life to be seen, not even on the horizon. Insects scurry over the red ground; they are the only animals to thrive in these conditions.

A fat, juicy ant makes its way over the fallen twigs of a dying shrub. Inches away from it, a lizard lies, motionless. It waits, as the ant approaches, unaware of its presence. The lizard darts forward and gobbles it up in an instant. It lies still as it works the ant down its throat, its hunger satisfied.

Suddenly, the lizard leaps to its feet. Its tail whipping around behind it, it scampers away, dashing off away from the shrub. Moments later, a large, clawed foot hits the ground near the bush, leaving a tell-tale three-toed print in the dust. The creature moves on, walking steadily across the land. Its feathers hang still in the breeze-less air and flies buzz around it. Banjo.

He is looking just as fit as the last time he was seen by his brother. However, his ribs are showing slightly; he has not been eating well. A short distance behind him, his mate follows. She, too, is hungry, and one of her fingers is swollen from an injury sustained during a fall when hunting. However, she still walks with confidence and pride as she strides along behind Banjo.

A third pair of footsteps can be heard on the dirt. A quieter, lighter footfall. A young, juvenile Australovenator. Only a little more than a year old, it is a bit smaller than an Unenlagiine. Its body is more lightly built than its parents, but it is still strong enough to accompany them on their trek.

The reason for Banjo and his mate's journey lies in the harsh summer. The heat and dryness of the land have driven a lot of the Ornithopods away, and the ones that are still here congregate in large groups, which are harder to sneak up on and ambush. This would be fine if it were just the two of them, but they have an extra mouth to feed, and a growing Australovenator juvenile needs a lot of food. There's just not enough prey in their lands for them, so they must expand their territory and explore new areas of their world.

And so their northward march began, and they are now nearing the edge of their vast territory. The choice to head north, however, was not a random one. There is a method to their march. To the south, east, and west of their territory are vast Australovenator ranges; the female knows this from her nomadic travels. And while there may very well be an Australovenator territory north of theirs, they remember that Swift headed north. To them, this means there is a chance that he found and staked a territory there; and Banjo knows that Swift is no challenge to him. The way they see it, Swift's land is not a place to avoid; it is easy pickings for them.

And onwards they march.

Chapter 5

Three days later. Flies buzz around the Savannasaurus carcass. Several flies circle around the female Australovenator's head as she lies on the sand. Grunting, she pushes down on the ground with her hands as she gets to her feet. The feathers on the underside of her body are caked with sand, and she trudges off into the sea. She moves deeper until it reaches her thighs, and then she lowers her body and feels the cool midday water lap against her stomach. She enjoys it for a few minutes, and then back off to the beach she goes.

She pauses by the carcass; no Ferrodraco have gathered. A couple are on the beach in the distance, but they have learned that trying to steal food from an Australovenator's kill while it is nearby is futile, and they pay it no heed. Content, she leaves the carcass. She marches through the cool forest to the creek, which is now so familiar to her. She takes a minute to replenish her thirst, having not drunk water in several days, and then she goes on her way.

The path that she now takes is one she has memorized, which she will never forget. A few minutes later, and she has arrived at the nesting site. In the clearing sits her mate. Swift looks at her, and bounds to his feet, joyous to see her again. They nuzzle, reunited after these long days apart. Then, Swift leaves, and she sits by the nest. She watches him go, as he heads off to their kill, casting a look back at her. Then he vanishes among the trees. She does not expect to see him again for another few days. She hunkers down, preparing for her vigil.

On the beach, Swift paces around the carcass, stretching his legs. Then, he sits by it, looking out to sea, where the Ferrodraco circle over the sparkling blue water.

Near the edges of the forest, an Unenlagiine scampers through the undergrowth. Suddenly, it hears a rustling of leaves and freezes. It is not alone. It looks around but sees nothing. Nervous, it lets out a high-pitched chirp. A second later, and the same chirp echoes out of the forest. Relief flows through the small dinosaur. It is just another of its kind.

It chirps again, and the other individual emerges from behind a cluster of ferns. The two greet each other, hopping around and flapping their little wings. Eventually, they calm down. With nothing better to do, they decide to move off together and turn to wander through the forest.

They freeze again. A rustling of leaves, and loud footfalls on the undergrowth. They each let out a single chirp. It is not returned. Nervous, they scatter, fleeing through the trees. Nearby, three large predators move. Banjo and his family have arrived.

The environment is new and full of interest to them. The dense undergrowth, of leaves and twigs, and the mottled colors of the ground, dappled with light and shadows, is brimming with novelty, but Banjo's attention is elsewhere. He and his mate have just picked up a scent. The smell of Australovenator.

Banjo turns and motions to his mate. She stops moving. Banjo then begins walking off. The juvenile starts to follow him, but the female lets off a low rumble. The juvenile pauses and looks at her. She sits down and lets out another low rumble – a cue for it to stay. However, the incredible curiosity of this young dinosaur is too great, and it continues walking after Banjo. The female gets to her feet and gently bites the juvenile on the back of its neck, pulling it back. The juvenile gets the message and stops moving. Banjo fades into the forest as he walks off; he will try to do this as quickly as possible.

In the quiet of the nesting ground, the female is sleepy, her eyes slowly closing. The calls of the Ferrodraco woke her up early today, but here, the stillness of the isolated clearing instantly calms her. And this dulls her senses.

A twig cracks and her eyes snap open. Suddenly, she is alert again, her parental instincts making her nervous, for her offspring's sake. She smells the air, and suddenly an odd scent presents itself to her. She sniffs again and begins to recognize it. And it fills her with fear. It is the smell of another Australovenator. Not Swift.

She gets to her feet and looks around her. She can smell it around her, but cannot tell where it is coming from. A fern's fronds shake, and she turns to try and find the source of the sound. A branch bending, twigs and leaves crackling. The female looks in the general direction of the noises. A shape comes into view, moving between the trees. Then, out into the clearing, Banjo emerges.

He walks confidently into the clearing, striding along. He looks her over; he can tell this is not Swift, but a new female. Even her scent is different from Swift's. A few thoughts flit through his head as he assesses the situation; perhaps she took over Swift's territory, or maybe this is his mate. However, those thoughts are fleeting, and a primal instinct settles in him. Not the urge to provide for his offspring, nor for his mate. Greed. The potential lands and food that are available. A territory defended by just one female is ripe for the taking.

He snarls. She returns the gesture. Banjo hisses, opening his mouth wide. He spreads his arms, baring his claws. He begins strutting around the clearing. Perhaps a show of strength will drive her off, and this will all be over. Suddenly, he notices something. The female is turning and positioning herself to face him, but in such a way that she is always guarding the area behind her. Sharpening his powerful eyes, he looks closely at what she seems to be protecting. He sees the telltale white ovals lying in the roots of the tree, visible beneath the green fronds covering the nest.

Eggs. The female has eggs. And Banjo knows a female will never leave her offspring. He snarls again, but this is not a threat. This is pure determination and energy, slowly seeping out from his body. And then his energy bursts out as he charges.

The female is caught off-guard as Banjo rushes up to her, mouth open wide. She is unable to dodge or retaliate, and his jaws close around her neck. She struggles, throwing her body from side to side. Banjo loses his grip, but he reacts quickly and bites down again. The female lashes out with her arms and scratches his shoulder. Realizing his attack has brought him within reach of her deadly claws, he lets go and backs off.

However, the female is now filled with rage and fear for her eggs, and she lunges without hesitation. Banjo rears back to dodge her first bite, but this exposes his neck. She lunges again, biting down around his throat. Banjo screams in pain and reaches up, grabbing her neck with his hands. Turning his body and shoving with his arms, he tears her off him.

She snarls in frustration. This proves to be a mistake, as Banjo takes the opportunity to take a swing at her head with his claws; she only just avoids them by pulling back. He slashes at her again, and she backs off. Now, she finds herself in the shade of the great tree, with her eggs only a few meters behind her. Her back against the wall, Banjo seems to have the upper hand. But this just means she has nothing left to lose.

She rushes him with her whole body and slams into him. Banjo stumbles back but keeps his footing. He then swings his body into her, and she staggers. He continues, shoving into her, shoulder-first. She snaps her jaws, trying to bite him, but her mouth can find no grip on his torso; it's like a dog trying to bite into ball.

And then her foot hits a root of the great Ginkgo tree, and it is all over. She comes crashing to the ground. Banjo looms over her, victorious. She snarls up at him and lifts herself slightly. He places his left foot on her chest, pushing her back down. She raises her head and hisses defiantly. Banjo bends down and, almost enjoying it, strikes her across the face with the back of his right hand. The smooth outer edge of the claws leave no marks, but the blow dazes her, and she slumps to the ground.

Banjo hisses and steps away from her. She lies still, gasping for air on the ground. And then he turns and looks into the shade of the great tree. Slowly but surely, he marches into the tree's shadow, and looks down at the eggs poking out beneath the ferns. Adrenaline pumping, the female lifts her head. Still lacking the strength to get to her feet, however, there is nothing she can do but watch as Banjo brings his foot up above the nest.

He slams it down on the eggs. In an instant, two of the eggs explode under the pressure of his foot, scattering yolk everywhere. The female screams. Banjo does not flinch and raises his foot again. Down his foot comes, and another two of the eggs are destroyed in a burst of yellow yolk and white eggshell. The female screams again, a pained cry, echoing out from her distraught core. Banjo inhales, in a low hiss, as he raises his foot for the last time, positioning it over the two remaining eggs.

An explosion, as something charges into the clearing, sending branches flying and crashing to the ground. Banjo turns, surprised, and sees, standing in the clearing before him, his brother. Twigs and leaves litter Swift's feathers, from his mad dash through the forest. He pants, out of breath, his heart beating wildly. He screeches loudly, accusing this attacker. Banjo then calls out—a low, deep warble. And that's when Swift realizes who he faces.

Memories flooding back, Swift lets out a high-pitched warble. Banjo is silent. Swift lowers his body and lets out a soft, almost inviting call. Swift still does not want a fight. Banjo lives for it. And so he screams, loudly, threateningly.

Suddenly, the female gets to her feet, Banjo's scream giving her new strength. Before Banjo can process this, she rams him sideways, slamming her right side into him. He stumbles, and retaliates instantly, biting down on her neck. She screams in pain as Banjo's teeth prick her skin and draw blood. His mate in pain, all thoughts of brotherly friendship end. Swift charges. Still occupied with the female, Banjo cannot react quickly, and Swift clamps down on his neck. Banjo releases the female, who backs off and stands over the nest.

Banjo swings his body to the right, slamming his head into Swift's neck and throwing Swift off. Rearing back, Banjo smacks Swift's head with the back of his hand. Dazed, Swift staggers, and Banjo bites down on the back of his neck. Swinging his weight to the left, Banjo throws Swift off-balance, and he falls down. Swift leaps up to his feet and takes a few steps back, regaining his footing. He snarls and snaps at Banjo's head, forcing the latter to back off. Swift's mate hisses, and Banjo realizes that the odds are no longer in his favor.

He calls out, loudly, a deep warble that echoes through the forest. A second call breaks out from deeper in the woods. Swift and his mate pause, surprised. A crashing of branches and twigs, and then Banjo's mate runs out into the clearing. She stands behind Swift, who turns to face her. Banjo then turns his attention to Swift's mate, hissing at her. She retaliates, snapping at him. Banjo reacts in kind, clapping his jaws together. The female screeches back, and the other two Australovenators turn their attention to the squabbling by the nest. Swift realizes the tension between his mate and Banjo is escalating, and he snarls at Banjo.

Banjo whips around and rushes him, snapping at his face. Swift dodges and swings his head into Banjo's lower jaw. Banjo hops back and then hisses angrily. With Swift distracted, Banjo's mate dashes towards him. Swift notices quickly and hisses at her, and she backs off. Swift glances towards Banjo, and then Swift notices his mate looking at him. Eye contact is made, and their bond reminds Swift of the nest and their legacy contained within. The only way to protect the nest is to draw the fighting away from the clearing.

Swift's mate hisses at Banjo, who turns and snarls at her. Grabbing his chance, Swift surges forward and bites on Banjo's head. Banjo throws him off, but Swift quickly swings the back of his right hand into Banjo's face. Swift then backs off, and Banjo strides towards him, pain running through his jaw. Swift shares one last glance with his mate and turns and flees, dashing off into the thicker trees. Banjo turns to Swift's mate, who still stands over the nest. He looks into her eyes, and she stares back with sheer defiance. Letting out one last snarl, he leaves her, running off into the forest after Swift. Banjo's mate glances at the female and then turns to follow her mate in the pursuit.

Swift crashes through the forest. A few leaves rustle nearby; Unenlagiines, disturbed by the commotion. Swift continues, drawn down the usual path between the clearing and the beach out of habit. A small clearing appears up ahead; running into it, Swift finds himself by the creek. He pauses for a second, catching his breath. He turns and looks behind him, waiting and hoping for the sound of Banjo following. A few seconds go by, and then a crackling of leaves and twigs betrays Banjo's pursuit. Swift calls out angrily, a loud hiss to reach Banjo's ears.

Banjo's silhouette appears between the trees. Fighting near the slippery creek would only increase the risks, and so Swift turns and runs, dashing across the stream and on towards the beach. Banjo soon reaches the creek. After a moment of hesitation, he splashes across the waters after Swift. His mate follows, with no hesitation. She, too, is determined to claim this land as hers.

Nearby, the juvenile Australovenator also scampers between the trees. It has heard the running, and, without its mother to restrain it, its curiosity drives it forward.

The big blue of the sea and sky becomes visible beyond the trees, and Swift runs towards it. The familiar feel of sand beneath his feet hits him as he leaves the forest and emerges on the beach. In the distance, the Savannasaurus carcass is beset by squabbling Ferrodraco, who decided to risk it in Swift's absence. Instinct and habit almost kick in, as Swift is tempted to rush towards the carcass and chase the Ferrodraco away. This thought vanishes a moment later, as Banjo rushes out onto the beach.

He stops and stumbles, unsteady on the soft sand. Swift does not hesitate to use this chance. He runs towards him and slams into him jaws first. He bites down on Bano's neck, and, unable to maintain his balance, Banjo falls down. Swift then whips around as a screech is heard behind him; Banjo's mate has arrived. Banjo rolls back and kicks upwards with his legs, catching Swift in the side as he is distracted. Swift staggers back. The female charges instantly, biting Swift's skull. He shifts his weight and tears himself free, and the female staggers on the soft ground. Turning to face her sideways, he rams into her with his right shoulder, and she falls.

Banjo, however, has risen up again. He runs towards Swift and hits him across the face with the back of his hand. Swift's ears ring as he is dazed, and Banjo follows up by biting Swift near the base of his neck. Before Swift can use his claws, Banjo has already let go, leaving Swift with a throbbing neck and no way to retaliate. Banjo then runs up to Swift's right side, and he swings his body towards Swift, ramming him in the ribs with his shoulder.

Swift holds back the pain and hops around, quickly changing his position to face Banjo's side. He bites down on Banjo's neck and swings his weight around, shaking Banjo and not giving him enough of a pause to reach up and slash him with those claws. Banjo hisses, unable to fight back. However, his mate comes to the rescue, slamming into Swift and causing him to lose his grip. Swift backs away, as the two Australovenators stand side-by-side and advance towards him.

In the distance, the juvenile Australovenator runs out on the beach. Much lighter than the adults, it has no issues on the sand, and it scurries out into the middle of the beach to watch the fight.

A little bit further away, the Ferrodraco squabble, arguing over the Savannasaurus carcass. Although there is plenty to go around, the larger individuals have monopolized the kill. They will not let the weaker ones eat until they have had their fill.

Swift continues backing away. There is nothing he can do now. Although, over the past year, he has gained enough experience as a fighter to take either of them on, he stands no chance against them together. However, he will not call for help. The only thing that matters to him is the survival of his offspring, and he will die for that if necessary. At least by taking a stand, he may hopefully weaken or even kill one of his opponents, and make it easier for his mate to protect the nest.

And so he screams at his brother. A challenge. One final battle. Banjo snarls in return, relishing the opportunity for a fight, and to show off his strength once more. Further out, the juvenile Australovenator watches, enraptured.

Swift charges, running towards Banjo. He lands the first blow, biting Banjo on the neck. However, Banjo's mate bites down on Swift, near the base of his neck, and the pain forces him to involuntarily let go. Swift breaks free and strikes the female across the face with his hand. He does not let her recover and hits her again, and again, the knowledge that his offspring will never be safe as long as they are here giving him strength. Suddenly, a massive pain causes him to scream in agony. Banjo has just slashed his thigh, driving his large claws through the flesh and leaving two great wounds. In pain, Swift does not react in time to stop the female biting on his throat, near his head.

Swift breaks free, and staggers back, limping. He then turns and glances to his side. Banjo stands there to his right, facing him. And Banjo jumps up into the air. Swift almost sighs, exhaling softly, as Banjo leaps, arching his back and once again aiming his feet directly at Swift's right side.

Swift closes his eyes and braces himself.

Banjo kicks out and hits Swift in the chest.

Swift topples backward. Broken ribs send pain even as he falls, with a second jolt of pain from his ribs as he crashes painfully to the ground. Winded and bleeding, Swift does not bother trying to raise his head in defiance. He cannot even muster up enough breath for a snarl.

Banjo's shadow falls over him. Raising his foot, he brings it down on Swift's chest, sending even more spasms of pain radiating out from the broken ribs. Swift screams a silent scream, with hardly any air in his lungs.

Banjo turns to his mate, who looks at him adoringly, with eyes full of approval. He looks down at Swift, who gulps in air in great breaths, trying to regain some strength, even though he knows it is hopeless.

Banjo has won. And he knows it. All Banjo needs to do is end Swift's life, and destroy the remaining eggs, and his takeover of this land is complete. Rearing back, Banjo lets out a scream of victory. A loud, guttural, primal call, spreading out across the beach.

The juvenile Australovenator relishes the sound. It cannot understand what the implications of this victory are, but its father's call conveys the sheer joy of it. And then the juvenile Australovenator makes the biggest mistake of its life.

It tries to mimic the call.

Its high-pitched shriek reaches his parents' ears, and they freeze. They look out across the beach and see the juvenile standing alone.

Its shriek also reaches the ears of a Ferrodraco standing by the Savannasaurus' carcass. Bullied away from the kill by larger, stronger Ferrodraco, it is hungry and frustrated. And it looks out across the beach and sees the juvenile standing alone.

One second and its powerful arms get it airborne at a dizzying speed.

Two seconds and it is halfway to the juvenile Australovenator, which is completely oblivious. Its mother screams, calling out to it. Banjo runs out towards it.

He dashes across the sand. 30 meters away. 20 meters away. 10 meters away.

The juvenile Australovenator suddenly gets the horrible feeling that it may be in danger. Sensing something behind it, it turns, just in time to see the Ferrodraco opening its jaws.

The Ferrodraco's jaws clamp down on its flesh. The pterosaur's momentum carries the young dinosaur into the air. Banjo is just three meters away from them, but the pterosaur's aerial agility is not to be underestimated. With a single flap of its wings, it shifts its body, in an attempt to dodge Banjo's final, desperate lunge.

Banjo misses. His jaws close on thin air, and it is all over. His brain still struggling to process what has happened, Banjo turns and sees the Ferrodraco flying off down the beach. Swift looks up, as the Ferrodraco's shadow darts across his face. The female Australovenator screams. She screams in an agony greater than that which any physical pain can inflict as her only offspring is taken from her, carried away from her at dizzying speed she cannot halt. All she can do is watch as her child's screams slowly fade away as the Ferrodraco sweeps it further and further away.

Stunned silence descends upon the beach. Banjo is still in shock. The female is wounded beyond belief. Her life has been shattered. Without even stopping to glance at Swift, she marches away from him, walking down the beach in the direction of the Ferrodraco.

Banjo slowly comes to. Seeing her walk away, he dashes after her, calling out. She stops. Banjo catches up to her. Together, they stare at the sky which has just taken their legacy.

Swift slowly clambers to his feet, pain still pulsing through his body. As he stands, Banjo turns and glances at him. In his eyes, there is no more hatred. No more emotion. Just defeat. The female turns and trudges off into the forest. Banjo and Swift lock eyes for a second, and then Banjo turns silently and follows his mate.

And onwards they march.

Away from the coastal forest, and through the barren desert. As the sun sets, the female stops. Banjo calls out to her. She remains silent. He approaches her and lets out a low, gentle call. She ignores him and turns her side to him. He lowers his head and begins nuzzling her, but she turns and snaps, letting out a harsh shriek. Banjo backs off, shaken. Tired and empty, the female turns away from him.

And onwards she marches.

Away from Banjo. Off into unknown lands. She has left him. In a single day, Banjo's greed has cost him everything.

And onwards he marches.

Alone.

Banjo and Swift

130

Epilogue

Banjo and Swift

Three weeks later. Deep within the forest, in a clearing, beneath the branches of a great tree, something begins to stir. A crack can be heard. Swift, still recovering from his injuries, jolts awake, nervous. However, this is not the cracking of twigs. It is the cracking of eggshells. Something is breaking out of the eggs. Swift lets out a high-pitched warble, waking his mate, who sleeps in the shade of a nearby tree. She approaches, and together they watch as the two remaining eggs start shaking.

An eye becomes visible as the creatures inside begin breaking through the polished white shell. A small head pops up; five times smaller than an adult Australovenator's claw, this is the head of a hatchling Australovenator.

In the other egg, its sister's tiny hand, which already bears minuscule glistening claws, breaks out of the shell. A few minutes later, and both of them are taking their first steps out of the makeshift nest, and towards their parents.

Two months later. The last of the night's stars are dimming as the morning hues start filling the sky. Purple, and then pink, with orange lining the horizon behind the trees. The sun then breaks over the treeline, and the beach comes alive with a soft yellow hue. As the Ferrodraco begin taking off for a long day of fishing, Swift and his mate step out of the treeline. They walk out to the water's edge and let the water lap at their feet. Between their legs, two juvenile Australovenators scamper. They run out into the shallows, jumping up and down in the water, joyfully splashing about.

Above them, Swift and his mate nuzzle each other as the sun begins to warm them. Swift has fully recovered; not that that has been a problem so far, as his mate has been able to provide all the food they could need. With their legacy running around in the water before them, they are truly content. For them, today, like so many recent days, will be a good day.

That night, the sun sets on a wild coastline. It will always have its dramas, and intertwining stories will continue to play out on these shores. For now, however, there is peace in this prehistoric world.

Banjo and Swift

Banjo and Swift

Bibliography

Flora of the Winton

McLoughlin, S., Drinnan, A., & Rozefelds, A. (1995). A Cenomanian flora from the Winton Formation, Eromanga Basin, Queensland, Australia. *Memoirs - Queensland Museum.* 38(1). pp. 273-313.
https://www.researchgate.net/publication/279907515_A_Cenomanian_flora_from_the_Winton_Formation_Eromanga_Basin_Queensland_Australia

Pole, M.S., & Douglas, J. G. (1999). Bennettitales, Cycadales and Ginkgoales from the mid Cretaceous of the Eromanga Basin, Queensland, Australia. *Cretaceous Research,* 20(5): pp. 523–538. https://doi.org/10.1006/cres.1999.0164

Dettmann, M.E., Clifford, H.T., Peters, M. (2009) *Lovellea wintonensis* gen. et sp. nov.- Early Cretaceous (late Albian), anatomically preserved, angiospermous flowers and fruits from the Winton Formation, western Queensland, Australia. *Cretaceous Research.* 30(2), pp. 339-355.
https://doi.org/10.1016/j.cretres.2008.07.015

McLoughlin, S., Pott, C., Elliott, D. (2010) The Winton Formation flora (Albian–Cenomanian, Eromanga Basin): implications for vascular plant diversification and decline in the Australian Cretaceous, *Alcheringa: An Australasian Journal of Palaeontology,* 34(3), pp. 303-323. https://doi.org/10.1080/03115511003669944

Australovenator

White, M.A., Cook A.G., Hocknull S.A. *et al.* (2012) New Forearm Elements Discovered of Holotype Specimen *Australovenator wintonensis* from Winton, Queensland, Australia. *PLoS ONE* 7(6): e39364. https://doi.org/10.1371/journal.pone.0039364

White M.A., Benson R.B.J., Tischler T.R. *et al.* (2013) New *Australovenator* Hind Limb Elements Pertaining to the Holotype Reveal the Most Complete Neovenatorid Leg. *PLoS ONE* 8(7): e68649. https://doi.org/10.1371/journal.pone.0068649

White M.A., Bell P.R., Cook A.G. *et al.* (2015) Forearm Range of Motion in *Australovenator wintonensis* (Theropoda, Megaraptoridae). *PLoS ONE* 10(9): e0137709. https://doi.org/10.1371/journal.pone.0137709

White M.A., Bell P.R., Cook A.G. *et al.* (2015) The dentary of *Australovenator wintonensis* (Theropoda, Megaraptoridae); implications for megaraptorid dentition. *PeerJ* 3: e1512. https://doi.org/10.7717/peerj.1512

White M.A., Cook A.G., Klinkhamer A.J. *et al.* (2016) The pes of *Australovenator wintonensis* (Theropoda: Megaraptoridae): analysis of the pedal range of motion and biological restoration. *PeerJ* 4: e2312. https://doi.org/10.7717/peerj.2312

Ferrodraco

Pentland, A.H., Poropat, S.F., Tischler, T.R. *et al.* (2019) *Ferrodraco lentoni* gen. et sp. nov., a new ornithocheirid pterosaur from the Winton Formation (Cenomanian–lower Turonian) of Queensland, Australia. *Sci Rep* 9: 13454. https://doi.org/10.1038/s41598-019-49789-4

Savannasaurus and *Diamantinasaurus*

Poropat, S.F., Mannion, P.D., Upchurch, P. *et al*. (2016) New Australian sauropods shed light on Cretaceous dinosaur palaeobiogeography. *Sci Rep* 6, 34467.
https://doi.org/10.1038/srep34467

Poropat, S.F., Mannion, P.D., Upchurch, P., *et al*. (2020) Osteology of the Wide-Hipped Titanosaurian Sauropod Dinosaur *Savannasaurus Elliottorum* from the Upper Cretaceous Winton Formation of Queensland, Australia, *Journal of Vertebrate Paleontology*, 40(3): e1786836-2.
https://doi.org/10.1080/02724634.2020.1786836

Poropat, S.F., Kundrát M., Mannion, P. D. *et al*. (2021) Second specimen of the Late Cretaceous Australian sauropod dinosaur *Diamantinasaurus matildae* provides new anatomical information on the skull and neck of early titanosaurs, Zoological *Journal of the Linnean Society*, zlaa173, pp. 1-65.
https://doi.org/10.1093/zoolinnean/zlaa173

Kronosaurus

McHenry, C.R. (2009) Devourer of Gods: The palaeoecology of the Cretaceous pliosaur *Kronosaurus queenslandicus*. University of Newcastle.
https://novaprd.newcastle.edu.au/vital/access/manager/Repository/uon:12164

Holland, T. (2018) The mandible of *Kronosaurus queenslandicus* Longman, 1924 (Pliosauridae, Brachaucheniinae), from the Lower Cretaceous of northwest Queensland, Australia, *Journal of Vertebrate Paleontology*, 38(5): e1511569.
https://doi.org/10.1080/02724634.2018.1511569

Isisfordia

Salisbury, S.W., Molnar R.E., Frey, E. *et al.* (2006) The origin of modern crocodyliforms: new evidence from the Cretaceous of Australia. *Proc. R. Soc.* B.273: pp. 2439–2448. https://doi.org/10.1098/rspb.2006.3613

Montefeltro, F.C., Bronzati, M., Langer, M.C., *et al.* (2019) A new specimen of *Susisuchus anatoceps* (Crocodyliformes, Neosuchia) with a non-eusuchian-type palate, *Journal of Vertebrate Paleontology*, 39(5): e1716240. https://doi.org/10.1080/02724634.2019.1716240

Winton Ornithopod

Hocknull, S., Cook, A.G. (2009) Hypsilophodontid (dinosauria: Ornithischia) from latest albian, winton formation, central Queensland. Memoirs of the Queensland Museum. 52(2) p. 212. https://www.researchgate.net/publication/288570399_Hypsilophodontid_dinosauria_Ornithischia_from_latest_albian_winton_formation_central_Queensland

Romilio, A., Tucker R.T., & Salisbury, S.W., (2013) Reevaluation of the Lark Quarry dinosaur Tracksite (late Albian–Cenomanian Winton Formation, central-western Queensland, Australia): no longer a stampede?, *Journal of Vertebrate Paleontology*, 33:1, pp. 102-120. https://doi.org/10.1080/02724634.2012.694591

Salisbury, S.W., Herne, M.C., Lamanna, M.C. *et al.* (2019) An exceptionally preserved small-bodied ornithopod dinosaur from the Lower Cretaceous (upper Albian) portion of the Winton Formation of Isisford, central-western Queensland, Australia, and the diversification of Gondwanan ornithopods. *Journal of Vertebrate Paleontology, Program and Abstracts 2019*, p. 185.

Miscellaneous

Hocknull S.A., White M.A., Tischler T.R. *et al.* (2009) New Mid-Cretaceous (Latest Albian) Dinosaurs from Winton, Queensland, Australia. *PLoS ONE* 4(7): e6190. https://doi.org/10.1371/journal.pone.0006190

Benson R.B.J., Rich T.H., Vickers-Rich P. *et al.* (2012) Theropod Fauna from Southern Australia Indicates High Polar Diversity and Climate-Driven Dinosaur Provinciality. *PLoS ONE* 7(5): e37122. https://doi.org/10.1371/journal.pone.0037122

Fletcher T.L., Moss P.T., Salisbury S.W. (2018) The palaeoenvironment of the Upper Cretaceous (Cenomanian-Turonian) portion of the Winton Formation, Queensland, Australia. *PeerJ*. 6: e5513. https://doi.org/10.7717/peerj.5513

Harrington, L., Zahirovic, S., Salles, T. *et al.* (2019) Tectonic, geodynamic and surface process driving forces of Australia's paleogeography since the Jurassic, in Keep, M. & Moss, S.J. (Eds), *The Sedimentary Basins of Western Australia V: Proceedings of the Petroleum Exploration Society of Australia Symposium.* https://www.researchgate.net/publication/335651775_Tectonic_geodynamic_and_surface_process_driving_forces_of_Australia's_paleogeography_since_the_Jurassic

Hocknull, A., Wilkinson, M., Lawrence, R.A. *et al.* (2021) A new giant sauropod, *Australotitan cooperensis* gen. et sp. nov., from the mid-Cretaceous of Australia. *PeerJ*. 9: e11317 https://doi.org/10.7717/peerj.11317

Van der Geer, A., Anastasakis, G., Lyras, G. (2014) If hippopotamuses cannot swim, how did they colonize islands: A reply to Mazza. *Lethaia*. 48(2). pp. 147-150. https://www.researchgate.net/publication/264461046_If_hippopotamuses_cannot_swim_how_did_they_colonize_islands_A_reply_to_Mazza

In addition, the skeletal reconstructions of Dr. Scott Hartman (https://www.skeletaldrawing.com/) and Henrique Godinho (https://www.deviantart.com/randomdinos) as well as skeletal reconstructions published in the above papers (notably Pentland et al. 2019 and Poropat et al. 2016), aided in the research and creation of the artworks contained herein (though the final pieces are not derivatives of any of their reconstructions).

Printed in Great Britain
by Amazon